LYNCHPIN UNIVERSE

THE ONCE AND FUTURE TWIN

OTHER BOOKS

Freckles: The Dark Wizard

Jam Sessions

Hold on Tight

Share Taxi: And Other Semi-True Stories

LYNCHPIN UNIVERSE

THE ONCE AND FUTURE TWIN

Jerry Harwood

Cover design by Keith Robinson

Dragonfire Press

Print ISBN: 978-1-958354-95-7

CHAPTER 1

When Kyle let his Maltese out to use the bathroom in the back yard, he did not expect to see himself bleeding to death. Or at least, a version of himself. Max, Kyle's Maltese, was less perturbed. Max flapped his tail as he ran down the porch steps. He then proceeded to bark at the boy who looked exactly like Kyle. Max licked the seeming identical twin before he spun, barked twice, and lay on his back to have his belly rubbed.

Doppelgänger.

That's what it was when you saw someone who looked like you. Kyle knew it from dress down day last year in ninth grade. He went as Albert Einstein, but it was obvious his wig and mustache were just a costume. This doppelgänger, however, was spot on. Kyle's doppelgänger grimaced as he took a blood-stained hand off of his side to pet Max. Kyle realized the boy in his yard, apart from looking exactly like himself, was dying.

His stomach had been sliced up the middle. The chainmail armor hanging down from the solid metal chest piece looked strong but was torn through like it was a cheap ripped T-shirt. Kyle shuddered at what could cut through chainmail. He glanced left and right off the porch, just in case whatever made that cut now lurked in the shrubbery along their chain link fence.

He saw nothing unusual except the oddly familiar boy in front of him. Kyle thought to spin, looking behind him to make sure the house door remained open. If things went bad and there was something nearby that had a taste for fifteen-year-old Kyle flesh, he would run back up the steps and into the house.

The air grew colder. There was no wind. In fact, the exact opposite. It was as if air was being strangled from the sky. Kyle had that feeling he got whenever he held his breath underwater a little too long. That moment of panic and a desperate need to be somewhere else. Anywhere else.

Kyle opened his mouth to pull in air and a cold rushed in, causing him to cough. The doppelgänger motioned him closer. Kyle stood still a moment, taking a few breaths through his nose. Even then the air was bitter cold.

Goosebumps formed on his forearm. Fearful, Kyle turned to go back up the stairs. He would close the door, then reopen it and all of this would be gone.

If not, he would go up to his room and shut the door. A good nap, maybe, and when he woke up everything would be alright. His backyard would be normal and it would again be a warm summer day in Chattanooga, Tennessee.

As he turned, Max barked. While he wanted to run up the porch stairs into the house, he couldn't leave Max out here. He called for the dog but Max paid no attention and continued to walk around in the grass near the doppelganger. He took a quick step to pick up his dog. Kyle's doppelgänger motioned again for him to come closer. Just as Kyle started to avoid the doppelgänger, snatch Max, and go, Max started doing the poop walk, sniffing grass looking for that perfect spot.

"Always perfect timing," Kyle said to the dog.

The idea of Max pooping on him as he carried the dog into the house caused Kyle to pause. At least Max seemed unconcerned by the doppelgänger. He took comfort in the fact the dog seemed okay with this very bizarre event. Kyle took three steps toward his doppelgänger and saw his insides were spilled out. What was the term his video game used in the subtitles?

Eviscerated. Yes, the doppelgänger's insides were eviscerated along the same slashed line where the chainmail was cut. Intestines oozed out on the recently mowed grass.

Now closer, Kyle could see the doppelgänger clearly. While the boy certainly looked like him, there were some obvious differences. That is, beyond the fact that Kyle's insides were still actually inside his body. The boy in the yard wore clothes that looked like Kyle's fourth grade Halloween costume.

That was the year he was obsessed with being a knight. Kyle's mom bought him a plastic breastplate, a plastic sword, and a plastic shield with a dragon sticker on the front. The doppelgänger laying on his back lawn wore the real thing. A magnificent chest piece with a red dragon stood tall in the center of the boy's chest. On his shoulders sat curved metal plates holding the image of a giant bear. His waist armor was covered by a thick, flowing blue and gold cloth draped between his legs.

The quality of the cloth was evident even now as it was soaked in blood. The leather boots looked hand-made, not the cheap kind massed produced to slip over a young kid's tennis shoes. The doppelgänger's outfit looked authentic, not like the one his mom bought at the costume store. Further, while Kyle had an athletic build, something he achieved with little effort on his part, he was nowhere near as muscular as this version of himself. No doubt about it, Doppelgänger Kyle was ripped.

"Where are you from?"

Kyle's voice cracked. It was a high-pitched voice he hadn't used since his awkward two years of puberty. Two years he thought were behind him. Puberty sucked. One minute you sounded like a cool action hero, and the next minute you sounded like *My Little Pony*. Kyle coughed and then tried again. This time his voice didn't betray him. "Who are you?"

"I am you." The words were followed by coughing and a splatter of blood along the ground. "You are me."

Kyle looked around the yard again. Maybe this was some elaborate prank. Kyle didn't know anyone that would go to that much effort to prank him. He wasn't that important, and he certainly wasn't popular, but he also wasn't unpopular. He just... was.

Naturally strong, no one bullied him but he never did any sports or sought out the spotlight either. And nobody in his school was going to go to this much effort to prank someone who just "was." He wasn't worth a note on his back or tripping in the hall type of prank, nor was he the kind of kid you made a sarcastic comment to. He certainly wasn't worth something this elaborate.

No, whoever this doppelgänger was, it wasn't a prank. Kyle confirmed his belief by looking around his privately fenced-in back yard. He realized the only people in sight were him and, well... the other him. No one else was there. This was not a prank. His doppelgänger moaned. Kyle turned his attention back to the strange encounter.

"How can I help you?" The *My Little Pony* voice thankfully stayed hidden. It is an oddity of being a teen that he didn't want to do something embarrassing, even in front of himself.

A scratchy but recognizable voice spoke in return. It was the voice Kyle heard whenever he listened to a video recording of himself. It was, indeed, his voice. Pained and dying, but distinctly his voice. It just wasn't coming from his mouth.

"Come here. I don't have much time."

Max barked. The dog, never earning the title "guard dog," apparently just noticed that he had not one but two people who looked like his owner. He looked at Kyle, then the doppelgänger. He let out another singular bark before walking over to his favorite number two spot with his tail wagging. Somehow, the dog's complete nonchalance about the whole situation continued to comfort Kyle who was pretty sure he was having a mental breakdown.

Kyle took the doppelgänger's outstretched hand. The doppelgänger's grip was incredible, almost crushing Kyle's fingers. Kyle grimaced, wondering how someone so hurt could still have strength enough to nearly pulverize his hand. He looked over the doppelgänger's wounds again. There was still no denying it. This boy was dying.

"You look, um, injured. I can call 911?"

Kyle looked at the intestines oozing out of the boy's stomach. He decided injured probably wasn't a sufficient description.

"Lean closer," the boy on the ground said. Then, with a difficult effort, he said louder, "I don't have much time left."

Kyle knelt beside his identical self. He was careful not to step in the blood-stained grass but felt his knee make a squishing sound as it landed in the earth. Something gooey seeped through his sweatpants. He tried to tell himself it was just where it recently rained but knew it hadn't rained in a week.

Time seemed to slow. Kyle's knee warmed with the oozing blood, saturating the cotton pants. The warm sensation made him aware his fingers were numb. It was still very cold. His nose ran a trickle of snot like he was outside in the snow rather than an eighty-degree August afternoon.

Kyle's thoughts were interrupted as his doppelgänger tugged his T-shirt and pulled Kyle's head inches from his own. The forceful pull almost made Kyle land on top of the boy. He stopped his fall only with an outstretched arm, planting his hand in some sort of intestinal goo.

The boy gurgled, a sound like using mouthwash except no mouthwash could cover the stench of air Kyle breathed in from the boy's cough. Blood flew out with the cough and landed on Kyle's "I'll role a D20" shirt. Kyle instinctually pulled away but his doppelgänger's grip was firm on both his arm and shirt. Very firm. Kyle was shocked this version of himself had such strength, even when dying.

"I am injured. Dying, in fact. I don't have much time. What I have to say... just listen to it. I am you, but not from this world."

"Like, from the future?" Kyle asked.

"No. Just listen. My time is short. I'm not from the future, but a different world. They are coming. In my world, they are already here. This world, your world, doesn't matter."

Kyle tried to pull back again but the grip held firm. He wanted to be offended at the words. Of course his world mattered. He lived in it. As did his parents, his friends, and even his annoying sister. Before today, Kyle hadn't even thought about there being another world unless it was in some movie or video game. This world, his world, was all he had.

The doppelgänger coughed before beginning again. Kyle thought he heard less strength in the voice this time. "Your world isn't a lynchpin. It is a single spoke attached to nothing. A dead-end path in a far-out hamlet. But the other world, my world, is a lynchpin world."

"My world doesn't matter? It matters to me!" Kyle said emphatically, gaining his courage. He pulled upward again. This time the hand released him. Kyle stood ready to protest. Then he paused. He was nothing special. Just a normal kid in a normal southeastern town in America. And if that was true of him as a person, was it crazy to think it might be true of a world, too?

Perhaps of a whole universe amongst other universes. Yet, hearing his doppelgänger say it made Kyle want to argue. He wanted to defend everything he had done. Everything he was. He thought about his achievements. His 5th grade science experiment that detected false coins. His complete playthrough of a video game last summer. His participation trophy not once, but twice in little league baseball. His Webelos cooking and survival merit badges.

Those personal experiences faded as he looked on his doppelgänger who most recently wore armor and fought a beast capable of ripping through him with ease. A doppelgänger capable of jumping through time. One whose strength suggested he could hit a baseball way past the infield. A version of himself who fought monsters rather than think about baseballs.

The doppelgänger's skin was splotchy and pale. His wardrobe spoke of a person of legend, like a noble character in one of his Dungeons and Dragons games. Kyle realized there was no defense to offer. Was he to tell this warrior version of himself, this man in a boy's body, that he got a B+ on his spelling test? Or that he was a level forty-seven in the video game UnderBlind? Or that his elf character in D&D had survived four campaigns? No. Kyle kneeled again beside the dying boy. This time there was no protest.

Max barked as he finished his business and began kicking dirt up with his back legs to cover his deposit. Kyle glanced briefly at Max and leaned closer to his doppelgänger. He was now within a few inches of the boy's mouth. Another wave of warm goo oozed through Kyle's sweatpants. Kyle heard Max give a single bark before spinning to look at his work.

Kyle looked into the eyes of his doppelgänger. They were his eyes, but hardened, bearing the weight of great power, great responsibility, and great importance. They were eyes that said "don't mess with me" even though the blood on Kyle's yard suggested someone did. They were Kyle's eyes, but Kyle was not the same caliber teen as this near-man in a teen's body.

"Who are you?" he said.

The boy's voice was raspier. Kyle could hear wheezing as the boy tried to breathe. "You need to find Merlin. Go talk to him."

"Merlin?"

"He lives nearby. He always does. He must live nearby. In all worlds, he lives nearby."

"Which house?"

"I do not know. In my world it is a cave with a stone in front of the entrance. Near the water. He always likes to be near the water. Find him."

"Um, we don't have any caves in my subdivision? And the only water is our neighbor's pool. But their names are McCorkles, not Merlin."

"Go village to village and ask. Go where the caves are if you must. Find him. Do this before all else."

Kyle thought a cave-to-cave search of his neighborhood would be quick. Whatever world this doppelgänger came from must be very different than his own. The boy's diminishing strength gave Kyle an urgency and boldness.

"Are you saying because someone comes and bleeds to death in my back yard, I have to go door to door like I'm selling girl scout cookies?" His sarcasm escaped his lips before he could think fully, a trait his mother suggested often would be his downfall. His initial fear of the situation was fading. It wasn't normal, not by any means, but his *My Little Pony* voice was locked away. Kyle was now feeling more in control, more anchored in this bizarre new reality in his back yard. He was feeling his sarcastic wit emerging.

This doppelgänger squeezed Kyle's arm. The grip was much weaker than before, though still stronger than Kyle could achieve. Probably not the person to be sarcastic with, even if it was a version of himself. Fortunately, the joke and hopefully the biting snark did not register. Odds are, this version of himself never ate a Thin Mint or even knew what a girl scout was.

"Find Merlin. This world," he coughed, "your world, is unimportant. But the lynchpin world... if it falls..." He coughed again, and another splatter of blood spewed. This time Kyle avoided being hit, pulling his hand free and standing again.

The boy on the ground gasped. With great effort he spoke loud enough Kyle to hear. "If I am not in the lynchpin world, if *you* are not in the lynchpin world, then it falls apart. All worlds fall. Find Merlin. Tell him to take you to the runes. From there, you must travel... to... the..."

The doppelgänger's words drifted into an eerie silence as his body went limp. Max came over. Perhaps he thought with two owners the result would be two beefy treats. He sat on top of Kyle's foot, looking back and forth between him and the stranger. Max then jumped backwards and let out two short barks.

Where the porch steps ended there was a small deck, big enough for the gas grill and a mop bucket. Oddly, neither the grill nor the mop bucket could be seen. All that was there was... Kyle didn't know how to explain it, exactly. It was as if the world was thinner there, as if someone had dropped one of those curtains you can almost see through.

It was like when he was a kid and would look at a bright light. Then, when he closed his eyelids tight, there would be an explosion of shapes and shadows dancing through his mind. Some held shapes similar to those he saw before closing his eyes but they would swirl, move, and become unrecognizable.

This was like that. He could see the shadow of a gas grill on the porch, but only because he knew what to look for. Otherwise, it would just be an unidentifiable shape. In front of it was a... what? Kyle could not immediately define it in his brain. He didn't have anything in mind that matched what this was. However, there was no doubt it was a terrible, menacing shape.

"Run." The voice, his voice, came booming to life in his head. Kyle felt a cold wave against his back like an ocean wave threatening to knock him down and drag him out to sea. Where would this thing drag him? he wondered. The feeling of ice water trickling down the back made him jump in surprise. The full body shake and resulting pivot probably saved his life as a lightning bolt came not from the sky but from the porch.

There was a flash of light, and Kyle used his forearm to cover his eyes. When he lowered it, there was a tentacle like the single arm of an octopus. Kyle couldn't see where the rest of the creature was. The tentacle just sort of appeared in the fog. A fog he didn't remember seeing moments ago but was definitely there now.

Kyle picked up the sword lying beside his doppelgänger. Without thinking, he slashed at the tentacle flying toward him. The blade stuck the tentacle, piercing it, and the creature recoiled. As it did, the hilt of the sword was ripped from Kyle's hand. It remained lodged in the retreating tentacle.

The fog lifted away like the smoke from firecrackers leaving the scene of an explosion.

The doppelgänger was ablaze from the earlier lightning strike. The stranger's body, still loosely recognizable, turned to ash. The ash rose into something Kyle could almost identify as his own image. It hovered in the air for a moment, then dissipated as it continued to rise.

Kyle waited to see the smoke dissipate, but before it did, it shifted. The doppelgänger was gone, but a new shape formed. It looked like an animal. Not one on four legs, though. One raised up on two legs with its head toward the sky. He had seen this image before when his family went to the Smoky Mountains. This one was... a bear? Yes, a bear on two legs made out of ash and fire.

The figure hung in the air over Kyle's backyard another moment before it turned into a formless smoke and disappeared into the sky. In less than a minute the sky was clear. All evidence of a tentacle and an invader from another world were gone except for a pile of ashes where the doppelgänger once lay and some charred grass.

Kyle looked toward the porch. He again saw the grill and the mop bucket, though the mop bucket was now overturned. He quickly moved to the porch steps and their relative safety before looking back over the yard. A circular breeze swirled over the ashes in the grass. It formed a small dervish and the wind pulled the ashes of his doppelgänger upward and away.

The breeze was cold. Kyle was reminded much of his shirt and sweatpants were wet. Yet, he watched the small tornado in amazement. It was not enough to cause harm to him or Max. It was just peculiarly targeted to the ashes.

A strange thought came to Kyle. If there were other worlds, perhaps the tornado on one world might be a light wind in this one. He pondered what kind of force would it take to shoot lightning from one world into another. It would have to be immense. Whatever that thing was that reached through from another world and lit Kyle's doppelgänger on fire was strong. Rip-through-chainmail strong, but even more so, it was rip-through-the-fabric-of-time strong.

The bloody handprint on his shirt and the blood splatter on his pants still remained. The grass where his doppelgänger once lay was no longer stained with blood. It was a faded brown, similar to a bald spot in a yard after a campfire. There was no indication it was recently the scene of a... what? A crime? A murder?

A death.

Max barked. Kyle watched as his dog marched over and sniffed the area before raising his leg and peeing. Satisfied, Max kicked his back legs, digging up a bit of dirt around the area so other dogs, rodents, and possibly other world invaders would know this was still his yard.

He lumbered up the stairs for his routine beefy treat. Kyle waited to see if Max disappeared into the strange thin layer of reality. It, whatever it had been, was gone and Max gave a single bark at the door to go back inside. Kyle followed Max inside.

CHAPTER 2

Kyle went to his room and took off his shirt. Under the words "I'll roll a D20" was a large twenty-sided dice. He stepped across the hall to the bathroom, turned on the faucet, and ran the shirt under it.

At first, the water was cold but quickly became warm. He turned it on as hot as he could get it and put a dallop of foam soap over each blood splatter, then folded the shirt with a clean area and rubbed the two sides together. After several minutes, all he had was a sopping wet shirt with blood stains all over it and bright red fingers that tingled as the feeling came back to them.

He looked at his sweatpants, knowing the same thing would happen with them. The stains on the knee would not rub out. They were ruined.

In a moment of panic, he looked around for a place to hide the clothes. Where would his mom not look? She was a laundry fanatic who would often come take his clothes out of the bathroom even while he was showering. Nowhere was safe.

As if to prove the point, his younger sister Libby burst into the bathroom. "Who was that in the backyard?"

"No one. Get out," Kyle said irritably.

"I heard you talking. Looked like fireworks too, or a fire!" She elongated the last word into two syllables. It was one of her signature moves any time she wanted to annoy him.

"I wasn't shooting any fireworks. Just mind your own business."

Libby grinned a mischievous grin. "Then what? I bet it wasn't a boy."

Kyle just stared at her.

"I knew it! It wasn't a boy. Was it Gwen from down the street? The one who you always stop to watch run. I bet it was Gah-When." Again with the double syllables.

"No. Get out."

"Sure, but I think someone has a girlfriend!" Libby stretched the word girlfriend out into its own sentence, then looked him up and down. "Hey, why aren't you wearing a shirt? Did she take it off?" Her smile got bigger. "Oooo."

Kyle picked up his soaked shirt and walked past her, slamming his bedroom door as she turned to ask, "Hey, why is your shirt all wet?"

Kyle decided it best to stash his shirt and pants under his bed. For extra caution, he tucked them beside a toy millennium falcon and an AT-AT. His mom wasn't nearly as fanatical about cleaning up toys as she was dirty laundry. He would have to get rid of them permanently, but this would do for now.

He walked over to his window and looked out at the back yard. He could see from his window the browned grass, scorched from the flash fire. The grass wasn't gone, but withered in roughly the same shape as a laid-out body. It was likely his parents would puzzle over what was killing the grass, and Libby would tell them he was playing with fireworks or starting fires.

He might even admit to doing it just to keep things simple. He'd get a scolding, but that would be it. Kyle thought they'd likely send him to a hospital to have his brain checked out if he told them what really happened. It would be a real stretch that his mom and dad would believe a version of Kyle from another world instantly burned up as he died. He barely believed it himself.

After throwing on a new shirt and some gym shorts, he went to his desk and grabbed a small pad of paper. Surely what he just saw was a dream. It couldn't be real. He wrote down the column of paper:

There is only one world.

Only one me.

I play sometimes as a knight in D&D, but I'm not one.

My sword is plastic and in my closet.

There are no octopus tentacles in my neighborhood.

There is no Merlin. No caves. No runes.

Lightning hit the back yard. There is a mark.

Maybe I passed out. Maybe it was just a dream.

He thought it was a good list. He read it a time or two, trying to convince himself that everything he saw was just a bad dream. Except, he wasn't asleep. It wasn't a dream. It was a bad... a bad what? Hallucination? Was he going crazy?

On the right side of the column he wrote:

Blood on shirt and pants

Brown spot in grass

Then in all capital letters he wrote and circled it three times:

I SAW HIM.
I HEARD HIM.
HE SAID TO FIND MERLIN.

23

CHAPTER 3

Kyle fell asleep on his bed holding the scrap of paper. His parents arrived home from work and the night's routine began. His mom woke him up and asked about his homework. He tucked the paper quickly under his pillow hoping she wouldn't ask him about it. If she did, he wasn't sure what he would say.

"Yeah, mom, this afternoon I saw myself in the back yard but my guts were ripped out and I was devoured in fire by a space tentacle from another universe." Somehow, "Not yet. I'll do my homework after dinner," seemed the safer bet.

Dinner was pork chops and rice. Kyle loved pork chops, but he hated that his mom always used pork chop night to renew her quest for greenery in their diet. There were never French fries or potato chips on pork chop night. It was always spinach, green beans, brussels sprouts, asparagus spears, peas, or kale. His mom would always say, "We are having rice and you don't need two starches."

Kyle walked over to where his mom was cooking to spy on what vegetable would plague his plate. As he did, his mom said, "How was your day, sweetie?"

"It was fine," Kyle lied. He still felt his insides twist and tumble as he thought about watching a version of himself die. However, instinct told him it was always best for a fourteen-year-old boy to not give too many details and not to sound too eager when giving out personal information to a parent. What would he say, anyway?

His thoughts were interrupted as his mom said, "You weren't downstairs when I got home. Were you really napping or were you playing those video games?"

"I fell asleep." That part was true. Then Kyle added, "I was trying to study. I have a biology test later in the week." That part was only partially true. He did, indeed, have a test.

"Good for you. Studying, I mean. Not sleeping. I always tell you that you need to study at a desk or down here at the kitchen table. Not on your bed. You study on that bed and you fall asleep. After dinner you can come down here and I'll help you. After dinner, though. Right now you can help me set the table."

As Kyle started to set out plates, Libby came down the steps. His mom asked her how her day went. Libby did not take time to answer before expelling her newest gossip. "Mom, Kyle was talking to someone in the backyard. I think he even caught the yard on fire!"

"Kyle?" his mom said with aggravation, looking over her shoulder. Her look let Kyle know his proclamation of study was now under suspicion. She stirred what looked to be boiled broccoli. "You said you were asleep. You know you aren't supposed to have anyone over when we aren't home. And never, ever play with fire. I always tell your dad that boy scouts is a bad idea."

"I wasn't talking to anyone," Kyle said. He looked at his sister and wondered if she had seen the backyard visitor or just heard him. "I mean, I let Max outside. Same as I do every day when I get home."

"I heard it mom! He let the dog out and then he was outside talking to someone. I think it might have even been a girl!" Libby giggled.

"Libby, did you see someone? Do you know who it was?"

"Mom, there wasn't anyone," Kyle feebly protested. He knew his sister would say whatever she wanted no matter what he did and that his mom would listen.

"No, I looked out the window from upstairs. But it was like, super foggy. Probably from all the fireworks and smoke. But I opened the window. I heard someone with like a high-pitched voice. Then the smoke came in and I closed the window real fast. I didn't want the house to burn down."

"It doesn't work like that," Kyle mumbled. Surely his sister didn't really believe smoke in the house would lead to a house fire. And of all the times she could've opened to listen in it had to be when his *My Little Pony* voice came out.

"Kyle," his mom said, "Is this true? Were you talking to someone? And fireworks? I really hope you weren't playing with fireworks."

"No mom, I was literally just talking to myself." Kyle thought that sounded better than an outright lie that he wasn't talking at all. He also thought his sister needed a punch in the arm for thinking his voice sounded like a girl. Kyle gave her a glare that told her as much. Then he watched his mom for signs she would push him for more. His mom always had a penchant for catching him in a full lie.

"Fireworks?"

Kyle didn't respond. His mom mercifully let the question go unanswered rather than leave it like a piece of dangling bait waiting to snag him with a hook.

On his way by the table, Kyle punched his sister in the shoulder. She shouted, but his mom ignored the cry. Kyle hated that he always had to set the table, clean up, and take out the garbage. Libby seemed to never have any chores. She was younger and, in Kyle's opinion, totally spoiled. He opened the fridge to get out the condiments. There, next to the oversized ketchup bottle, was a box of thin mint cookies.

Kyle popped one in his mouth, making sure his mom was still focused on the stovetop. The cookie reminded him of the recent girl scout cookie sales his sister participated in, and his comment to his doppelgänger about doing door-to-door visitation looking for a Merlin.

He decided to try and bring up Merlin to his mother. He thought maybe Libby's door to door cookie sales were his best path forward. He checked his mom was not paying attention, popped another thin mint in his mouth, finished it, and then asked, "Mom, can I have a few thin mints?"

The expected answer. "Not before dinner."

Kyle wiped his mouth in case there was any remaining evidence. "OK. After dinner then?"

"Only if you eat your broccoli. You and Libby don't eat enough vegetables. We are going to start having a green vegetable at every meal."

Kyle ignored the vegetable lecture. He had a more pressing agenda and now was his moment. "When Libby sold these, did she go door to door? You know, selling cookies?"

His mom stopped and turned around, holding her spatula. For a moment Kyle thought he didn't set up the question well. Or perhaps she was onto the fact he already had two cookies before dinner. He tried to find a place to look other than his mom's all-knowing eyes.

Then his mom spun back around. "Why, yes. She went around the neighborhood."

Kyle hesitated. The next question he wanted to ask was risky. It might cause his mom to stop cooking and take more interest in Kyle's afternoon adventure. Yet, he wanted to know. He needed to know like in a Dungeons and Dragons game, sometimes it was just worth the roll of a dice in hopes you came up lucky, he tossed the next question out. "Do we have a neighbor name Merlin?"

His mom stopped stirring. She waved the wooden spoon in the air, tapping each house on their street as she looked over the invisible map in front of her. "There is a Mr. Merle Olson at the end of the street. Right next to the McCorkles. Very unkept yard. A real eyesore. I hate it for Mrs. McCorkle. Homeowners have spoken to him several times. It doesn't seem to do any good."

"And his name is Merlin?" Kyle felt his mom was missing the point of the question.

"His name is Merle, not Merlin. Were you hoping we had a wizard as a neighbor?"

Indeed, he was. Maybe. Or maybe he was hoping he wasn't and everything that afternoon had been a bad dream.

I SAW HIM.

I HEARD HIM.

My doppelgänger was real.

Kyle looked at his mom. She was hardly considering if real wizards lived in the neighborhood. Her smile told Kyle that he was okay to press forward. She took his question to be the harmless fun of a boy who loved wizards and dragons. So, he pressed.

"Do you know him?"

"Not really. I remember his name because it is the same as the actor on *Little House*. Coincidence, I'm sure. Definitely isn't the real Merle Olsen. He died a few years back. Wonderful man. Wonderful show. I always loved that show. You know, that is the problem today. You are always playing those violent games and Libby is always watching those God-awful sitcoms. Most of those shows she watches don't even have parents in them. Just kids running around, doing whatever they want. And don't get me started about those video games your dad lets you play. No wonder—"

Kyle interrupted her. He really didn't want her to get started on a rant about video games, for a lot of reasons, but primarily because he wanted to know more about Merle Olsen. It wasn't quite Merlin but it wasn't so far away as to not be Merlin either.

"Do you ever talk to Mr. Olsen?" Kyle asked it with a little more force than he intended. However, he needed to know if Merle Olson could be a Merlin, not hear his mom's oft given lecture about better choices watching television or playing games.

"What? Oh, no. We met him when we moved in here before you were born. He bought that house and moved in the same weekend. Your dad went down thinking he might make a new friend. Not a lot of families move in to this area, you know. So, he thought meeting the other new guy might be good. Your dad came home saying Mr. Olsen was nice but a bit odd. More interested in the types of trees in the neighborhood and how one was blocking the view of the moon than who would win the Tennessee game that weekend.

"And your dad said Merle smelled peculiar. Like fresh Christmas trees and peppermint even though it wasn't anytime near Christmas. We haven't talked to him since. His yard is overgrown and he put in an odd fence all around his place. It's made out of different fencing material and sometimes what looks like random scraps of junk. An eyesore. And right in front of the neighborhood. When he is outside where you can see him, he is always... well... he is a bit peculiar to say the least. We certainly didn't let our precious Libby go there selling cookies."

"So, he's outside sometimes?" Kyle asked. His mom stopped stirring and turned to him. Kyle felt a lump in his throat. He had overplayed his hand.

"Why the sudden interest?"

Kyle tried to quickly come up with an excuse. The best he could offer was "A friend of mine said there was a guy here named Merlin. Just didn't know if it was true."

"A 'girl' friend," Libby said, making the word girl two very loud and long syllables.

"It wasn't a girl. It was one of the guys at Epik Games, where I play Dungeons and Dragons on Friday nights."

"You boys. No, sorry to disappoint. All we have is a guy named after a *Little House* actor. And one whom you'd be best to leave alone."

Libby cut in. "Mom, did you, like, have the hots for him? I mean, the character on *Little House*?"

"Oh, no. I mean, I had a few TV crushes, but not him. He was old even then. In fact, I wouldn't be surprised if Mr. Olsen's parents named him after that guy. He was pretty famous even outside *Little House*. Merle played football in the sixties before he was on the show. Isn't that crazy? A football player starring in a family show? Wouldn't see that today."

Kyle set a fork and knife beside each plate at the table. When he walked around Libby's spot, he took a moment to punch her in the shoulder as only a kid brother can do.

"Ow! Mom!"

Kyle's mom never looked back as she said, "Kyle, don't hit your sister, even if you are just teasing. Chivalry may be dead in the world out there, but not in this world."

Kyle dropped a fork. It clattered to the ground. "Mom, did you just say, 'not in this world?'"

"Yes," she said, not looking up from her pot. "My world. My house." She waved the wooden spoon over her shoulder at him. A piece of broccoli fell off and Max scurried over to see what had fallen. He took a sniff of the green vegetable, turned up his nose, and walked away.

Kyle's mom scooped up the fallen piece and threw it in the trash. She took the broccoli off the stove eye and checked the oven to see if the pork chops were done. She looked up from the oven's puff of steam and shouted, "Dinner's ready! Kyle, go tell your dad."

Kyle's stomach lurched at the thought of dinner. He could not get his mind off what he had seen or what he was asked to do.

CHAPTER 4

Lance sat next to Kyle in social studies. He was Kyle's best friend since the two met at NoogaCon in elementary school. They spent the weekend playing an introduction to Dungeons and Dragons with an occasional break to the video game room. Ever since, they were inseparable unless a teacher with a seating chart got in the way. While several teachers ensured they sat on different sides of the room, Mrs. Langston had always allowed them to be together, even though it meant she was constantly telling the two boys to be quiet.

Kyle opened his social studies book per instructions to study but he couldn't focus. Instead, he doodled in his notebook: *Lynchpin world. This world doesn't matter. My world matters. Find Merlin. Find the Runes. Find...??????*

He doodled the words in the margin, allowing the question marks to trail off the edge of the page. Around the words, Kyle drew in his talented hand pictures of his doppelgänger bleeding on the ground. Then he drew a picture of an old man surrounded by stone runes. Then a tentacle reaching around the page's upper margin. The picture came to him as he drew it. It was like a part of his brain already knew what wanted to be there in that margin. What needed to be there.

Lance whispered, "What are you writing? New D&D stuff?" He leaned over his desk toward Kyle's, risking Mrs. Langston's tongue lashing. "Those drawings are cool! Like the best you've ever drawn. What is it?"

"Nothing. Just scribbling." Kyle flipped the page so Lance couldn't see it anymore.

Lance just reached over and flipped back to the page with artwork. "What is a lynchpin world? Sounds cool. And that wizard by the rocks is like the coolest thing you've ever drawn. You ought to draw him bigger, like on his own sheet of paper or something. Or make him a character for D&D."

"Thanks. Yeah, maybe I should."

"Did you draw him from something you saw?"

"It's just something... I'll tell you later." He turned the page so the scribble was not visible.

Mrs. Langston looked up from her desk and gave a stern "Shhhh!"

At recess, Lance was quick to ask again. "That stuff you were writing about. What is it? D&D? From a new video game or a card game? Or a board game I don't know about? I haven't seen any games called Lynchpin."

"Um, sort of," came Kyle's reply. He regretted putting his thoughts on paper. Yet, he couldn't help himself. Since the day he saw his doppelgänger, he found himself constantly writing lists trying to talk himself out of what he saw and heard. However, for every time he wrote out his list, an image came to mind so clear that it was easy to draw. And every time the voice in his head screamed, "I SAW HIM. I HEARD HIM. FIND MERLIN."

And this voice wasn't his normal voice nor the treacherous *My Little Pony* squeal. It was from deep within him. It was, he came to believe, from the space in himself that, in another world, allowed him to be the mighty knight that threatened to crush Kyle's hand. The version of himself who held no fear in fighting horrific beasts or jumping into new worlds.

Lance continued to stare at him. He tried to shuffle off the question, but Lance kept waiting. Pushing away his thoughts, and added, "I mean, it must've been something I saw recently."

Lance didn't let it go. He wanted to know where Kyle got the idea and image. "Oh cool! It isn't on Xbox, is it? It's probably on your phone. That would make sense why I haven't heard of it. My parents took mine away. Not my fault. They never told me I couldn't be on it after midnight. Apparently, I should have 'just known common sense.' They just told me to put it up at night, but after twelve starts the next morning. Totally unfair." Lance paused to let Kyle nod his agreement. Kyle did so though his smile was forced. This conversation made him uncomfortable.

Lance pressed, "So, is it a cool game?"

If there was anyone Kyle could share his experience with, it was Lance, but even his best friend wouldn't believe him if he told the truth, that he had been visited by another version of himself. That he had watched that version of himself die in his backyard. Kyle decided to tell another half-truth, a small, white lie. "What if I told you it wasn't a game. It was something I saw. Like, you know, a dream."

"A dream?" Lance asked.

Kyle left the question hanging officially unanswered, but allowed Lance to conclude Kyle had a vivid dream. Indeed, Lance asked for details and Kyle told Lance all about his meeting of his doppelgänger and the cryptic message. He gave every detail, except that it wasn't a dream. That part Kyle kept to himself.

"That is the craziest, coolest dream ever!" Lance said. The bell rang and the two started to move toward the door where the line was forming. "And those are the best drawings you've ever made. That wizard is a total stud. You said it's Merlin? Like the one in—"

"King Arthur," Kyle interjected. He wanted to slap his forehead. King Arthur. Of course, Merlin was the wizard in King Arthur. That is where Kyle knew the name. He would have to add that piece to the left column of his notepad, now titled "Reasons I Am Imagining All This."

"Wouldn't that be cool if there was a dude named Merlin that lived in your neighborhood? You know, and was like a wizard. I mean, wizards are really strange and scary, but still. Who wouldn't want to meet one?"

Kyle paused to let a few other students through the door before stepping into the hallway. "Yeah," he said. It did sound cool if you were Lance and absorbed in video games,

Netflix movies, and D&D games. It was a lot more scary than cool if you were Kyle and saw that tentacle in your own back yard.

Yet, talking to Lance helped Kyle think about it as a dream or a kid's wild imagination. After all, he and Lance spent almost every Friday night at Epik Games playing Dungeons and Dragons. And this story just seemed like the kind of thing a Dungeon Master might concoct to start an adventure. However, there was still one problem. That one line on his little scrap of paper:

I SAW HIM.
I HEARD HIM
FIND MERLIN.

CHAPTER 5

That Friday night, Kyle's dad dropped him off at Epik Games, a local comic and game shop in a strip center across from the town's mall. His dad would go to a coffee shop or the mall food court and do some work after getting Kyle some fast food.

Kyle waited near the comic racks until Lance entered the store. This was the core of their friendship. Two young adventurers who loved a good story and lived life by the roll of a die. Epik Games always had a crowd on Friday nights. There was Magic, Pokemon, board games like Settlers of Catan, miniature games like Warhammer and, of course, Dungeons and Dragons. The two friends made their way to the back room where there was a weekly game of Dungeons and Dragons for fifteen and under adventurers.

Lance was quick to tell their regular dungeon master about Kyle's drawings.

"Emory, Kyle drew some cool pictures this week. A rad looking wizard and this tentacle thing. You should totally use it in a game."

Emory set his pizza box down and took his backpack off. "Got them here? Always cool to see what you guys are drawing," he said, pointing a finger at Kyle. "Especially you. You've got talent."

He flipped open the lid of the pizza box and grabbed a slice of the 16 inch pizza, taking a bite. He would buy one every week at the pizza place next door. Pizza was his life, or at least that's what he would tell the boys. The game would last a few hours, as long as it took him to eat the whole pie. When he finished, he would speed the game to a breakneck pace and bring it to a close. That fast-paced adventure at the end was Kyle's favorite part.

Until then, Emory coached and helped the players, especially whenever there were little kids joining with their moms in tow. He would make sure the whole party made it safely to the end, even if it meant someone got to reroll or suddenly found a revival spell on the floor of the dungeon.

At the end of the game, once the pizza was gone, anything was possible. Emory didn't care if the dragon, golem, or witch destroyed each player or not, so long as the game came to its conclusion. That thrill and risk was the best part of the evening.

Emory put the crust in his mouth and stretched out his hand. "Let me take a look."

Lance nudged Kyle and he pulled the art pad out of his bag. Kyle's face turned a little red. It was awkward being praised for anything, but especially this. He still didn't want to talk about it. He wanted to convince himself it never really happened. The left column of his list was getting longer:

I was tired that day.

The cold could've been because the backyard is more in the shade.

The brown grass could just be grass that was mowed too short.

Libby says she looked out the window and saw fog.

She would've seen the tentacle arm.

But the left column still held those three compelling lines:

I SAW HIM.

I HEARD HIM.

FIND MERLIN.

Kyle unzipped his backpack and set his potato chips on the table. Emory flipped through the art pad which was now nearly full.

And, if Kyle were honest, the art was getting better. His talent was improving. He wasn't taking any classes or anything, but each time he drew an image from that day, especially the tentacled creature, he saw it more vividly in his mind. That in itself was disturbing, but he also realized he could draw it with superb accuracy. It was more like tracing a picture than it was freeform drawing, even though the original was only in his imagination. Or was it…

I SAW HIM.

Emory set down the art pad. It was open to the last page with Kyle's most recent drawing. In it, the tentacle took prominence, entering the side of the page in landscape style. The word 'Lynchpin' scrolled through the tentacle like it was part of the scales. The fallen body of the doppelgänger sat beneath the tentacle with smoke rising as his shield caught fire. The smoke rose up and into a bear shape. In the upper right was a wizard emerging from a cave entrance with a staff in hand.

Emory took the drawing and studied it. His eyes flickered and for a moment Kyle only saw white in his eyes. It was as if they rolled backwards. The blue returned, and Emory handed the paper back. Kyle started to ask if

Emory was okay, but he spoke before Kyle could say anything.

"So cool," Emory said. "I mean, really cool." He was a local college kid Epik Games paid a few bucks each week to lead young kids through a game. Kyle knew Emory's presence every Friday night was a side hustle, but he was still an adult and one that Kyle looked up to. "So cool," went a long way.

"Kyle said it was a dream he had," Lance added.

Another kid at the table interrupted them. "Are we playing our old characters tonight or do we have to make new ones?"

Emory ignored the question. He looked at Kyle and took a swig of his energy drink. Emory's gaze turned to a focused glare. His eyes flashed all white again, just for an instant. Then Emory smiled and handed the pad and loose picture back. There was a long pause, perhaps ten whole seconds. The younger players practiced rolling their dice. Kyle ignored a D10 that plopped into his area. Instead, he continued to stare at Emory, especially watching his eyes. There were no more flashes of white, but Emory finally blinked.

"You know why I started playing? I mean, what first got me into D&D?" Emory smiled broadly and took a bite of pizza.

Kyle shook his head.

Emory continued. "I was about your age. At the time I was all about TV and video games. Knew a few people who rolled the dice but never thought about joining them. Then I saw something." Emory paused to let the statement sink in. Even the two younger kids joining the game sat still.

"I later told everyone it was a dream. Heck, twenty years later, I think I convinced myself. But you know what? There is a part of me that knows what I saw wasn't a dream. What I saw that day, I mean. There is a part of me that still thinks it was real."

Kyle felt his *My Little Pony* voice rise up as he said, "Really?"

Emory didn't seem disturbed by the high-pitched reply. "Yeah. It was over there actually."

Emory pointed across the street to the mall and its two-story parking garage. "They were building the mall back then. I know… I'm old… like almost twenty-five now, but I remember my parents talking and grumbling. The build was going too slow or something. Over budget and behind. Apparently, there was a real problem. In the news—back then families all had the news on when we ate dinner—they showed where the concrete slab they built sunk into the ground. Then they poured it again. It sank in a second time. My dad drove us over to see the twisted metal swallowed up. Everyone said it must be a sinkhole or something. That was the story on the news also."

"That's cool. A sinkhole that swallows up the whole mall," one of the younger players said.

"Yeah, but that wasn't even it. So, like I said, my dad drove us over there like we were going to a theme park or something. He wanted to see it for himself. We even parked and walked up to the chain link fence that surrounded the work site. It was then that I saw it. Inside the sink hole, if that is what it really is."

"What? What did you see?" Lance asked before Kyle could speak.

"When I was over there that day, I saw..." Emory paused, dramatically making eye contact with everyone at the table before continuing. Even the younger kids trying to spin dice on their edges stopped to listen. "I saw in that hole something incredible. You know what it was? It was a white dragon. It was hidden amidst all the metal scrap and the dirt. It was sleeping, like a bear hibernating in the winter. But that dragon..."

Emory looked toward the mall. It was quick, but Kyle saw Emory's eyes flash all white again. He thought Emory could still see that dragon the same way Kyle could still see the tentacle. Kyle wondered if when Emory's eyes flashed it was similar to what happened to Kyle when he saw a blank portion of paper. An image just appeared so clear and exact that it was like he was in the moment. Perhaps Emory was seeing that dragon again this very moment.

"What did you do when you saw it?" one of the younger players asked. Emory had the young kids on the edge of their seat with his story. He also had Kyle totally immersed in the tale, though for different reasons. The middle schoolers were enthralled in what they thought was a cool dragon story. Kyle, however, had an inclination that Emory was talking about a real-life dragon.

Emory continued, "I told my dad. Twice. He just dismissed it as the imaginings of youth. He patted me on the head. He said I had a great imagination. Then we went back to the car and drove to get hot dogs and ice cream. By the time I finished my scoop of strawberry, I thought my dad was probably right; it was just my imagination. But there was a part of me that thinks different, even to this day. There is a part of me that knows I saw it."

Kyle's hand drifted to his back pocket where his list sat.

I SAW HIM.

I HEARD HIM.

FIND MERLIN.

Kyle tried to form a question. He wasn't sure what to say. How could he tell this adult man, a few years further down life's path, that Kyle saw something, too. How could he tell Emory about the tentacle and that it wasn't a dream but real? Very, very real.

How could he tell Emory about Kyle's doppelgänger dying and that it might have even been a version of King Arthur even though it looked just like Kyle? How could he tell Emory that weird things happened, and that the dragon Emory saw all those years ago might be real and maybe even from another universe? A lynchpin universe.

What would happen if he did tell Emory? Would he believe him? Or would he laugh and dismiss it as childish fantasy? Maybe he would pat Kyle on the head like Emory's dad did to him. Or maybe he would stop and nod his head and listen. In some ways, that would be even worse. Then Kyle would have to admit to Lance that his supposed dream was real. Or at least that Kyle thought it was real. Lance was likely to believe his best friend had gone crazy.

Besides, there was a part of Kyle's own mind that desperately wanted to believe everything was just his imagination. To believe that if he just kept living life like normal, it would fade away in his memory. Indeed, Kyle thought that was maybe the best path. To force himself to put it out of his mind. To forget it.

Kyle's thoughts circled back to the group's conversation as another kid at the table jumped in. "So how did they fix the mall? I mean, it doesn't collapse anymore, does it?"

Emory looked up to the young man. Kyle thought he saw Emory shake his head as if to shake off the memory. Kyle wondered too if Emory tried to pretend it was just his imagination. Maybe that was why Emory was such a great storyteller, a fantastic Dungeon Master. Perhaps it was because he could tell a story so good he could convince himself it was false even if it wasn't. Kyle considered this for a moment. Maybe that is what Kyle needed to do.

Emory grinned. The storyteller in him brought his arms and legs to life. He rose out of his seat and leaned over the table, telling the next part standing up.

"They moved the plans for the whole mall to the left. Then they built pillars and put the parking garage over that area. It looks like the garage floor sits on the ground, but if you look closely, you can see it doesn't. It sits on pillars away from the area that kept collapsing."

"Oh, gotcha. That's cool," the kid said. Then, apparently more interested in the dice in front of him than a parking garage, he asked, "So, do we have to make new characters or can I use my level four elf?"

The game started and nothing more was said. Emory finished his pizza and brought their game, an adventure through the woods to save a small village from Wood Woads, to an end. Kyle's knight survived the tale only by the help of Lance's character who tossed him a flaming sword at just the right moment.

The night ended without further mention of tentacles, wizards, or dragons. But that night, Kyle went to sleep and for the first time in days thought about something other than his dying doppelgänger. He thought about that white dragon that surely still lived under that parking garage.

Kyle knew, though he had no idea how, that the dragon was now awake.

CHAPTER 6

Few things took Kyle's mind off his worries the next few days, but it was not for a lack of trying. Kyle exerted great attention to pushing the bizarre events out of his mind. One thing that surely helped was the opportunity to see Gwen run. Gwen was a year ahead of him and Lance at school. She had long legs built for running and the start of cross-country season meant she ran laps through the neighborhood several days a week. Her blond hair would bounce in a ponytail as she ran through the cul-de-sac in a sports bra and runner's shorts. Kyle made a point on Saturdays to mow whenever she was out practicing.

This week his timing was perfect as he turned the riding mower around the side of his front yard and toward the road's curbside just as she came around the corner to their street. He ran the mower along the very edge of the curb, watching her move gracefully along the road. Less graceful was when he drove the front wheel off the curb.

In a panic, Kyle lurched the wheel back to the yard. The result was the mower bucked, suspended for a brief moment on the two wheels now in the street, and then tipped over. Kyle toppled off the seat onto the pavement as the seat spring triggered the engine to shut off.

"Are you okay?"

The world was a bit blurry. Kyle wiped his brow and realized his hand was now red. He folded the bottom of his shirt up to wipe his face. It came away red as well. His stomach churned as he thought about the day he saw a version of himself with blood everywhere, dying in his backyard.

While the doppelgänger was attacked by some crazy space monster and Kyle was only attacked by an off-track lawn mower, he couldn't help but think about the connection. If what he saw was real, then Kyle might meet the same end. He shuddered. Kyle forced himself to look down at his legs. He was bleeding, but not nearly enough to die. His legs and arms were covered in a bright crimson rash from the asphalt. Some areas sprang little streams of blood, trickling their way down.

"Are you okay?" came the voice again. It was soft and sweet.

Kyle smelled a wonderful scent. It was like the vanilla candles his mom burned. He looked in the direction of the smell to see Gwen in her sports bra smiling down at him. Even with her hair pinned back in a ponytail, sweat gleaming on her forehead and out of breath, she was the most beautiful person Kyle had ever seen. She even smelled good when running, something Kyle knew he could never achieve.

"Dude, like seriously. Are you okay? That was a nasty wreck. You have a concussion or something?"

"I'm... I'm okay."

"What happened?"

Kyle knew he couldn't say he was too busy watching her run to pay attention to the curb in his own front yard. All he could offer was, "The mower," as if the mower became a sentient being and ran him off the curb rather than his own clumsy self. Whatever chance he had with Gwen, which was admittedly none, was now none squared to infinity.

Still, she took time to help him stand up and put his arm around her shoulder as he limped toward his front porch. There was even a moment where she joked with him saying, "I just got my license. You let me know when you get yours. I'll stay off the streets."

Kyle began imagining the peculiar dream only a teen boy can have. What if this actually was the moment where Gwen fell in love with him. They become high school sweethearts and marry after college, building a family and enjoying trips around the country together. All of this came in a flash as he felt her strength under his arm leading him to the door. In spite of the facts, he again imagined there might be the hope of a romantic spark.

However, it all went away when his mom came out the front door yelling, "Kylie-poo. Oh, my dear sweet boy, are you okay?"

Kyle's cheek flared hot as he limped inside. Behind him he heard his mom telling Gwen how thankful she was for such a sweet young lady to be their neighbor and how her Kyle has always been one to get hurt. Kyle at least convinced his mom to close the front door to stop the embarrassment before she tried to help him stop the bleeding. The rest of the night Kyle couldn't decide which hurt more, his body or his ego.

The next day at school, Kyle knew his woes about his doppelgänger would be outweighed by the heckling of "Kylie-poo" in the hallway.

After all, who was he kidding. Gwen was a cheerleader and popular. And a kid who couldn't run a mower named "Kylie-poo" was easy fodder for bullying. He was certain by the time she ran home his nickname was posted everywhere on social media for everyone to see. Kyle gritted his teeth, waiting for the heckling to start as he made his way to his locker.

Lance came over to Kyle's locker as he was closing it to go to first period. "Dude, what happened? You look like you got in a fight with a pit bull. Or..." Lance's voice went quiet. "Or... was it... like, you know... a tentacle or a dragon?"

"Nothing like that," came a voice behind Kyle's locker door. He closed it to see Gwen's smile. Her perfectly straight teeth flashed as little dimples appeared on either side of her lips. "More like a lawn mower."

"I, uh..."

"I got this one," Gwen added. "He was looking at this pretty girl running by and drove his lawn mower off the curb."

"I mean, I didn't—I..." Kyle felt his face heat as his cheeks turned red.

"I think that about sums it up. Gotta say, I've had a few boys fall for me, but never one literally take a fall." She giggled, pressing her

Chromebook and notepad to her chest. Kyle closed his eyes, waiting for the, "See you soon, Kylie-poo." However, it didn't come. What did happen was Gwen's lips met his cheek.

"Gotta say, you are kind of cute yourself. Even if you are a bit scratched up right now." She giggled again and walked away. A few steps later, she was side by side with two other girls talking about something other than Kyle and Lance.

"Dude," Lance said. "Gwen is like the hottest girl in school. And she just kissed you."

Kyle opened his mouth but no words came out. He was comfortable being a nobody, another kid lost in the shuffle. It was better than being bullied or harassed. It was better than being someone at the bottom of the social ladder. He always accepted that as his lot and never aimed for much else.

But today, for the first time ever in his life, Kyle thought he might be able to go the other way. Instead of going from a ghost no one noticed to a loser that is bullied, he might go from unnoticed to popularity. After all, he just got kissed by Gwen. He felt a bit of pride in his limp as he walked to math. Visions of a life with Gwen danced through his head the rest of the day. It was a much nicer set of thoughts than

large tentacles invading his back yard and
killing people.

59

CHAPTER 7

The next Friday, Lance spent the night with Kyle. The two arrived at Epik Games to find out Emory was out sick. They spent a few minutes waiting to see who else showed up before abandoning the effort. There were a few other games to join, including a new release Pokemon tournament, but the boys opted to cross the street to the mall where there was a one-price-for-an-hour arcade featuring old video games.

"Maybe Dragon's Lair is working," Lance suggested. Kyle could tell Lance shared his disappointment about D&D being cancelled.

"If not, we can play all the way through Gauntlet Legends," Kyle offered.

Lance nodded vigorous agreement. "As long as I get to be Valkyrie."

"Always stealing the girl from me," Kyle laughed.

He sent a quick text to his dad to tell him the new plan, then sent another one confirming the two boys made it safely across the street and into the mall's main hallway. They stopped to grab some pretzel bites and headed to the arcade. There they paid their money and walked around the thirty or so games. Dragon's Lair had a line around it as it always did on Friday nights. Gauntlet Legends was also occupied. However, in the back the owner had a small section of pinball machines. A recent addition was Dungeons and Dragons from Bally. The boys took to it.

"Not as good as an adventure, but still pretty fun," Lance offered after thirty minutes. The two finished their rounds and moved over to Super Off Road. "Still, what I wouldn't give to see a real dragon. You know, like Emory saw."

Kyle looked over at his friend. "Do you think Emory was telling the truth?"

"Why would he lie?"

"I don't know," Kyle said, perhaps with a bit too much sarcasm. "Maybe to impress a bunch of teens and a few elementary age kids there to play Dungeons and Dragons."

"Nah," Lance said dismissively. "I saw something in his eye. He was telling the truth. Besides, we're already impressed. I mean, we look up to him. He already knows that. He's the best Dungeon Master in town by far."

Kyle pondered this a moment, stopping to do so in the middle of the walkway. Lance stopped, too. A woman pushing a stroller almost ran in to him. She glowered as she swerved the stroller around the two boys. "You boys should be with parents, not in the way of everyone. There should be a curfew. Next thing you know kids like you will just be running around in the streets doing whatever you want. Lord knows what trouble you'll get into then," she muttered under her breath.

Kyle ignored the jab and looked at Lance. "You really believe him?"

"His eyes. When he talked about it. I don't know, but they—"

"Went all white," Kyle finished.

"Yeah, just for a second. Maybe less than a second. And then, I don't know, I just felt he was serious. Like, take a lie detector test to prove it serious. Almost like he was looking across the parking lot at that parking garage and could still see it. That makes me crazy, doesn't it?"

Kyle shook his head. "No. I don't think it makes either of us crazy. I saw him do it, too."

There was a pause, and then he decided to take the risk. "Lance, I have to tell you something."

He was thankful his voice was strong. The *My Little Pony* voice crack would've made his confession sound weak.

"You know how I told you about my dream?" Kyle waited until Lance nodded. "Well, I wasn't asleep. I mean, I think it was kind of like what Emory said. I think I actually saw it." He looked at Lance to see his reaction. His best friend looked on with interest and trust. If there was anyone Kyle could come clean with and admit the truth to, it was Lance. He stated his next words clearer than he had to anyone.

"It wasn't a dream. I really saw it."

Lance looked at him. Kyle couldn't tell if the gaze was one of doubt or awe, but finally Lance offered a hint of a smile and said, "Seriously?"

"Yeah, is that crazy? I mean, am I crazy?"

"Let me see your art pad."

Kyle rummaged through his backpack and pulled out the pad with the pages of drawings. Lance flipped through them as he walked over to the few tables scattered around for those eating in the food court. He unzipped his own bag and pulled out a D&D book. The cover had a white frost dragon blowing ice instead of fire across the page. The title was "Monsters of

63

Dungeons and Dragons. "You mean, you saw something that might be in one of these books but in your back yard?"

Kyle thought he heard doubt creeping into his friend's voice. He couldn't blame him. Kyle doubted it, too. Except:

I SAW HIM.

I HEARD HIM.

FIND MERLIN.

"Yeah. I mean, not the dragon, but that tentacle." Kyle pointed at his drawing of the tentacle with a sword stuck in it recoiling into the portal in the sky. He looked again at Lance's eyes to see if his friend still believed him.

Nervously, he offered, "Or maybe not?" He was letting the doubt come back into his own mind. "I mean, it wasn't a dream, but maybe, I don't know, like a hallucination or something. It probably was nothing."

Kyle waited. Lance continued to look at Kyle's art notebook and also skim through his Monsters of D&D book, then he closed both. His finger ran across the spine of the D&D book and over to the cover. He tapped the cover twice hard making a *thump, thump* before handing the art pad back to Kyle. "Your dad isn't picking us up for another thirty minutes. Let's go look under that parking garage."

Kyle agreed as much to move the conversation away from his own experience to Emory's. He didn't want to crawl around an outdoor parking garage at night, especially when his dad thought he was inside the mall.

Still, if Emory's experience was true, it would go a long way in convincing himself that his doppelgänger needed him to travel to other worlds. And if it was just a normal, old parking garage, as Kyle hoped and expected, it would affirm the whole thing was just Kyle's too vivid imagination.

I SAW HIM.

I HEARD HIM.

FIND MERLIN.

The words written on Kyle's paper back in his room seared his mind. If that dragon was in the parking garage and Kyle and Lance did find him, then Kyle would have more trouble denying the dying words of his doppelgänger. And if he did have to go find Merlin, maybe if Lance saw the dragon he would join Kyle. He considered this possibility as the two made their way outside.

The covered walkway to the garage had a low guardrail at the end. The two boys slipped under and down a small embankment to the hedges that ran along the structure. Lance hit Kyle on the shoulder, pointing out the window at the foundation. "It really does look like it sits on the ground from the road. But here it's clear it doesn't."

Lance pointed at the two-to-three-foot gap. There was a space between the false wall and the start of the garage. A gap, just like Emory had told them. The gap ran along the entire side of the garage hidden behind overgrown hedges.

"Give me your phone," Lance said. Kyle handed it over with the screen on. He considered it was a sign of true friendship when you could hand over your phone to someone without question. He trusted Lance.

Lance turned the flashlight feature on. Both boys walked behind the first hedge, pushing the branches out of the way. They lowered to their bellies and crawled through the gap. Underneath was enough space to crawl on their knees because the ground descended. Further in, the ground continued to slope downward. The garage was built over a pit.

Lance scurried a bit further, spinning his feet around. He slid on his bottom until he could quasi-stand. His feet dug into the ditch's side and his hands extended out to support him. He shined the phone downward. "This thing goes down a long way."

Kyle looked over where Lance shone the light. He could only see a few more feet down before there was only darkness. "How do you know? I can't see how far it goes. I can't really see anything beyond a few feet."

"It is definitely a pit underneath. From here I can see it gets real steep," Lance said. "Come down here and look."

Kyle joined Lance on the ditch's steep incline. He took back his phone and scanned around. Suddenly, the area filled with light. Headlights shown through a gap in the hedges across the way where cars came to a four-way stop. The headlights let the boys see much further than the phone's light allowed.

They waited a minute until another car arrived. The vehicle either had to have low headlights or the light didn't penetrate the hedges and parking garage wall. Soon enough, they got a chance to look again under the shine of more headlights. With a little better idea of the terrain, the two maneuvered a bit further across and down toward the far end of the parking garage.

There they saw a tube. It was like the ones used by roofers when they reroofed Kyle's house a few years before. More of a chute than a tube, really. Lance made it there first since he had taken the phone back. The world around Kyle went totally dark as Lance raised the light inside the chute. "It's concrete. They are pouring concrete in here." Lance's voice sounded like a young boy at Christmas opening exactly what he wanted.

"Makes sense." Kyle noticed his own voice creeping a little higher. He controlled it before continuing. "I mean, if it is a sink hole. They must drive the cement truck up here to the backside and just pour in concrete."

Lance shown the light and the two boys could see the chute went a good distance down. Kyle lost his balance. He only slid a few feet, but in so doing he reopened his road rash on his arm. Bright red blood immediately came to the surface.

"You okay?" Lance asked.

"Yeah, just slipped. No biggie." He took his thumb and rubbed the bubble of blood off his skin. Then he flicked it downward into the dirt before looking to see how much more blood might surface.

There was a rumble and the ground beneath the boys shook. The cement chute next to them gave a loud crack as some part of it below snapped or splinted into fragments. Lance grabbed Kyle's shirt and yanked upwards. "Let's go!"

The garage shook again. Below, the darkness turned to light. Except, that wasn't quite right. It didn't light up so much as glow. A white, cool, radiant color. A cool blue. There was a fissure in the concrete. Kyle didn't know the word at the time, but heard it later on the news when a reporter said it was just a simulated earthquake from the sinkhole and everything would be okay.

But it wasn't okay. Inside that fissure was a small but very real white dragon. It was maybe six feet long at best. The glow was coming from it, and as it spread its wings, the whole sink hole lit up.

Another few drops of blood spilled from Kyle's arm and some dribbled onto his pants. The dragon turned as if the blood hitting the ground was an alarm to check. It gave a screech and flew up the hole. The air all around Kyle and Lance turned cold, dropping several degrees. The dragon hovered in place a moment, looking at the two boys.

The dragon didn't speak exactly, but Kyle knew the voice he heard inside his head was the dragon's voice the same way he thought Jedis knew when dead Jedis talked to them in Star Wars movies. It was not just inside his head, but all around him.

"You must hurry."

Then it turned and flew away. Where the dragon once hovered, there was a blue light. Kyle tracked the dragon as it flew low beneath the concrete of the parking garage floor. It landed on the opposite side and another blue light appeared as it worked its way out from under the garage. There was a loud cracking sound as the dragon lifted a section of the garage up for his escape, then it was out of their sight. Kyle heard a horn blast outside, a car crash, some screaming, and then all went quiet.

The two boys shuffled out from under the garage. As they did, it gave another groan. The side where the dragon exited gave a loud crash as the pillar holding it collapsed. The garage tilted, and Kyle and Lance watched in awe as cars slid toward the falling pillar. The garage collapsed inward. It was like something out of a movie, except this was not from any special effects.

"I hope no one was hurt," Kyle said.

"We could've been killed," Lance added. The point was made clearer as the pillar nearest them cracked and the corner sank a few feet. "We should get away from here. I mean like further from this thing."

A security guard blew a whistle making the point even clearer. He motioned for the boys to follow him and waved the crowd into the street for safety.

Lance grabbed Kyle's shoulder. He winced in pain, but looked at his friend.

"Kyle. We just saw a dragon."

Yes, they did. This would have to go on his list.

I SAW HIM.

I HEARD HIM.

FIND MERLIN.

I SAW MYSELF FROM ANOTHER WORLD.

AND NOW A DRAGON.

A DRAGON. LANCE AND I BOTH SAW IT.

CHAPTER 8

Kyle's phone started buzzing as his dad tried calling. He was at the coffee shop down the street, but within minutes, his car pulled up. Kyle's dad slammed it into park, set the emergency lights to flashing, and jumped out. "Are you two OK? Are you hurt?"

Kyle became aware that he and Lance were covered in dirt. They probably looked like they had been in the very center of the disaster. Kyle assured his dad they were fine.

"I'm glad. How scary. Come on, let's get away from here."

The boys got in the car. The only conversation was Kyle's dad's declaration, "Let's go get some ice cream before we head home. I think we could all use some to wind down a bit."

Kyle and Lance gave nervous looks to each other, both knowing it best to wait until they got to Kyle's room to unpack and think about everything they saw. And what it said. Except that wasn't quite right. What it thought? What it sent. Yes, that was right. What it sent to their minds.

A scoop of vanilla did help him calm down. Kyle played the scene over and over in his head until his dad turned the car into their neighborhood, where a scene pulled even the attention of a young boy who just saw a dragon away.

His dad slowed the car. "What in the..."

Kyle followed his dad's gaze from the driver's seat off to the left. It was the McCorkles' home, and their swimming pool in the back yard was lit up with an eerie green light.

"Are they having a pool party?" Kyle asked.

"I don't think so. I don't see any lights on." His dad slowed the car almost to a stop before adding, "In fact, I think I recall Gibbs saying they were out of town for the weekend."

"Then what is that?" Kyle pointed to the pool barely visible through the lattice fencing. The answer came as Kyle followed the green light from the pool across the yard. In the next yard over, the green light gathered as if it was a school of fish swirling. It was graceful, almost hypnotic. Kyle knew from television such gatherings of fish were fragile. They would scatter at any fright or scare. He felt this gathering of light was much the same.

The car lurched forward a bit as his dad committed to a full stop. As if the car's cessation sent an unseen pulse, the light lifted and scattered. A dull glow remained, and in the middle of the it was an elderly man. He looked to be in a bathrobe and was howling.

Kyle rubbed his eyes. Yes. Howling. Kyle's dad must've thought the same as he rolled down his window just a little bit. The warm summer air poured into the car along with a "Owwwwooooooo." He rolled the window up immediately.

"Dad, what is that man doing?"

"That's Mr. Olsen. Who knows. Best we not bother him. He might be..." Kyle's dad paused considering what words to use. Whatever words he originally considered were set aside for safer ones. "He might have drunk a bit too much."

Kyle's parents never drank and neither did their friends, but even without real life examples, television had a lot of drunk people in it to watch and observe. None of them that Kyle could remember had ever gathered green light from a neighbor's pool and howled at the moon.

"You have some weird neighbors," Lance said in a whisper.

The words carried to the front seat where Kyle's dad heard it. Feeling the need to respond he said, "Well, just the one. Mr. Merle Olsen. But I suppose he is odd enough for five neighborhoods. I'm sure the homeowner's association will give him a call tomorrow."

Lance leaned over to Kyle with wide eyes. "Merle Olsen. Like Merlin? Maybe that is, like, who you are supposed to go see?"

Kyle turned his head back toward Mr. Olsen's yard. The green light was beginning to gather again and he thought he heard another howl. Kyle couldn't be sure, but he thought he heard a single thunderclap. The green light didn't scatter this time. Instead, it pulled up and into the air like there was an invisible vacuum cleaner sucking it out of the sky.

When the last of the green light left, Mr. Olsen's yard went quiet. Kyle tried to see if he could see anything or anyone in Olsen's yard but it was dark. There was, however, a fox or something similar walking along the sidewalk under the lone street lamp. Kyle strained his neck but his dad's car drove past a neighbor's house and Kyle's view was blocked.

CHAPTER 9

The next morning, the boys went out in the neighborhood "just to walk around." Kyle's dad then conscripted them to "take your sister and get her out of my hair." Libby insisted on walking Max on the leash as he went yard to yard marking his territory. Kyle found himself getting agitated with his sister. He wanted to get to Olsen's house and see what was going on in his yard. He also wanted to see if the green aura was still there, and maybe even see Merle Olsen himself.

There was a "yip, yip" as Max broke free from his leash. Libby lunged after him, stumbling, and falling on the ground. Kyle and Lance took off after Max, who ran with surprising speed straight toward a neighbor's front porch.

Once there, Max turned and hiked his leg, letting the world know he claimed the porch column in the name of all Malteses everywhere. Kyle beat Lance to the dog and scooped him up.

When he turned back to where Libby was, he saw two guys in his grade talking to her. Except they weren't exactly talking.

Wallace and Gabe. School bullies who happened to live on this end of the subdivision. One was walking around Libby in a circle while the other was pointing at a place in his yard where Max recently pooped. Libby, always feisty, moved her lips and tried to walk away. Gabe pushed her back and Wallace stepped in closer.

Gabe continued to point at the spot in his yard, then he pushed Libby down. It wasn't a hard push, but it didn't take a much to push an elementary age girl down when you were on the other side of puberty. It didn't matter how hard it was, he'd still pushed her. No one pushed his sister around except him.

As annoying as she was, Kyle would do anything to protect her from jerks like Gabe and Wallace. Not that Kyle was some kind of macho hero. He knew going over meant he would more than likely get beaten up, but better him than Libby. Kyle set Max down and ran toward his sister.

Ten seconds later he lowered his shoulder into Wallace. The two tumbled onto the ground. Kyle felt his scrapes from the lawnmower incident open back up. He rolled on top and took a swing at Wallace's face. The punch went into his cheek as Wallace turned. Kyle raised his hand for another go when he felt himself lifted up and off his feet. Gabe, easily three inches taller than Kyle, held him in a bear hug. Gabe arched his back to make sure Kyle's swinging feet couldn't find purchase on the ground.

Kyle felt a punch in the abdomen and suddenly it was difficult to draw in breath. The arms gripping him released. He was still gasping for air as his right leg buckled under him. A kick connected with his chest.

He knew he had to do something before he fell to the ground. But what? The answer came as Wallace sent his foot into Kyle's stomach. He pulled his arms against his side and winced as another foot struck him in the arms.

A surge of energy washed over Kyle. It was like cold water running in reverse up his spine. He had never felt anything like it before. Yet, there was some part of him that thought the surge was always there, always in him, just waiting for the right moment. Today must've been that moment. He let out a roar and pushed Wallace's foot up and away.

The effort sent Wallace's leg upward at an unnatural angle. Wallace didn't just stumble backward. He lifted several feet into the air as he turned, landing hard on his stomach. Kyle hadn't just pushed him off, he'd sent him into a flip like some kung fu movie.

Kyle rolled to his knees. He still felt the pain still in his stomach, but it had diminished. Seeing Wallace writing on the ground, Kyle felt confident to stand. He turned toward Gabe, who pointed at Kyle but didn't make any movement toward him. He pounded his fist into his palm and announced, "Let's do this."

"Do what?" said a voice.

The voice was neither Wallace nor Gabe's. Nor was it Lance's or Libby's. It was a girl's voice. Kyle swung his head, keeping Gabe in his peripheral vision. Standing in her running shorts and sports bra, with a protective arm around Libby, was Gwen.

Wallace snarled at Kyle. "Your dog took a dump in my yard. Your little brat of a sister just left it there."

Kyle lowered his defense a little, glancing first at Gwen then back to Wallace. "I'll scoop it if that's the issue, but do not push my sister." He stood waiting to see if the two bullies would take his offer as compensation. They could walk away with their pride and feel they won by making him pick up dog poop. That was fine, so long as they left Libby alone.

Wallace looked over his shoulder at Libby and Gwen. Being one of the prettiest girls at school, if not the prettiest, had certain advantages. Her displeasure was just as powerful as any punch or kick to the gut. She and Wallace locked eyes for a brief second before Wallace broke contact, looking down at his shoes. He turned back to Kyle. "Nah. I don't want your pansy butt on my property. Just keep your dog off it, and your sister, too." With that, he waved to Gabe and the two walked away.

"Your pansy butt took him down to the ground," Gwen said with a smirk once the two bullies walked out of earshot. Kyle loved the dimples that showed when she smiled. "You know, you flipped that kid straight back. You ought to join the football team next fall with skills like that."

The football team. Kyle was athletic enough. It wasn't the athletic side of sports that he avoided; it was just that he never felt like he was important. Somewhere along the way, he became comfortable not being the lowest in his school's popularity structure but not being in the highest bracket, either. He was comfortable being in the middle where no one noticed him.

It had advantages. He could play Dungeons and Dragons or card games and no one cared or bullied him. He saw jocks do that sometimes to other kids. And if he wasn't an athlete, no one would expect him to be a bully. He knew a few who were nice enough, but just as many weren't nice at all to the kids on the lower end of society at his school.

The middle was the sweet spot. Kyle was just a ghost, an irrelevant member of his school. And thus, he had never considered sports an option. Or at least, he never did until now. He never did until Gwen, the girl he overturned a mower trying to watch, told him he should.

He considered it for a moment. He wasn't weak, although he wasn't strong either. Maybe he could be an athlete. If so, he could hang out with Gwen and her amazing dimples all the time. His mind drifted again to the land of imagination where he and Gwen were together. She was the star cheerleader, and he the quarterback. A goofy smile crossed his face.

"What is that smile for, handsome?" she asked.

"I just might."

"Might what?"

"Just might join the football team."

Kyle noticed Lance now stood behind him with Max in tow. "Me too, maybe," his friend said without much confidence. "I mean, maybe I could try out, too. You know, maybe."

Gwen looked Lance up and down. Kyle felt just a small twinge of jealousy as she did it. Then she smiled at him and said, "I bet you could."

Kyle felt a little flusher in his cheeks. Was he actually jealous of a girl whom he had no relationship with smiling at his best friend? Perhaps. Either way, it was clear the path to be friends with Gwen led through the football coach's office. He diverted Gwen's smile to Lance by saying, "I think I just might do it. Go out for the team, I mean."

"Oh, good!" Gwen said. Her smile and dimples returned their focus to Kyle. "Coach will be glad to have someone who can toss a guy that far off the line." She pointed to where Wallace landed in the dirt a few moments ago, then walked over and stroked his arm with her fingernail.

"And it'd be cool to see you on the practice field every day. You know, the cheerleaders practice out there at the same time. But either way, a man who protects his kid sister is OK in my book." Gwen gave Libby a hug, then turned back to Kyle and winked.

A clear, deliberate wink. Kyle felt that wink had more power than any push or shove from Wallace. Gwen put her earbuds back in before starting her jog away. The two boys and Libby watched as Gwen made her way down the street and up the hill to another section of the neighborhood. Max barked twice to be let down. There were still many more yards to conquer for a dog determined to poop or pee in each one.

CHAPTER 10

Kyle and Lance went to Coach Edwards the next school day. Coach gave them both a consent form. That night at dinner, Kyle slid the form across the table to his dad. He calculated the moment when his mom was still putting food on the table and his dad was relaxing in his designated chair at the table.

"Dad, I thought about signing up for this. Is it okay? And if so, I need you or mom to sign it."

Kyle's mom set down some rice. "What is it?"

His dad looked over the form and set it down with a huge smirk. "My boy! I knew you had it in you. Just like your old man!"

"What is it?" his mom asked, this time with a little more urgency.

"Football! Our boy wants to join the football team. Season already started, I suspect?"

"Just a week or so. Coach said we could still join."

"We?"

"Oh, Lance is joining too."

"You boys might get hurt," his mom protested. However, it was a weak effort. It was clear Kyle's dad was going to make sure Kyle had a signed form the next morning.

The following afternoon Kyle was put in pads and taught how to buckle his helmet. He wasn't a quarterback, but the coach determined he had the speed and size to be a linebacker. Lance was going to try his hand at defensive end, which meant the two got to practice together on defensive drills. Lance also worked Tight End drills. On Wednesdays, Kyle had to tackle him as he caught passes across the middle of the field.

The next two weeks went by quick between school and practice. Kyle's bruises and scrapes from the lawnmower incident healed. However, new ones multiplied with each day of practice until, finally, bumps and bangs started hurting less. As Kyle's dad proclaimed to his mom's continued protests, it was just Kyle "toughening up."

Kyle didn't get to play on Friday night, not as a sophomore who barely knew the plays, but he got to dress out. It also meant he and Lance missed Epik Games and any chance to talk with Emory again. They looked for him on their social accounts, but couldn't find his profile.

After several weeks of new friends and new school status, the urgency of asking Emory's opinion of their mall encounter diminished. So did Kyle's interest in meeting his odd neighbor, Merle Olsen. Kyle was enjoying popularity. And popularity had rules to follow. Talking about tentacle monsters destroying your doppelgänger or your eccentric neighbor being the wizard Merlin were not part of the accepted conversation starters anymore.

A part of Kyle knew that it was crazy to keep silent. What he and Lance saw in that parking garage was so much more important than the all-you-can-eat buffet after their away game. What they saw was monumental. It was bigger and greater than anything a normal school day had to offer. However, there was an intoxication about a routine where he was popular, growing some muscles, and getting to talk with Gwen and the other cheerleaders.

He and Lance occasionally brought up the subject when talking in private, but neither suggested they skip a game night to go play at a game shop. They simply chose a new life as football players that didn't allow for that kind of thing.

Instead, their conversation revolved more around whether they would also try out for the basketball team in a few months. Besides, the mall disaster was determined to be faulty construction according to the news, not a dragon.

It soon cycled off the news report Kyle heard each morning as his mom drove him to school and was replaced by more important stories such as the town's budget increase for road repair the next year or the therapy dog Salvation Army was using to help homeless vets.

The voice in his head reminding him of his doppelgänger quieted to a mere whisper. The whole event in his backyard started to fade from memory. Maybe it wasn't even real. Maybe it was the fanciful imagination of a kid who still played Dungeons and Dragons on a Friday night instead of a young man who proudly stood with his team on the sideline. He was maturing, and needed to set aside such things.

Emory, who Kyle once saw as a mentor and role model started to seem more like a sad man who never got to grow up like Kyle was doing. After all, those games were for kids. He liked being popular. He liked being an athlete, liked that Gwen smiled at him in the hallways and even sat with him at lunch on Thursdays when their schedules aligned. His world was normal

The world of doppelgängers, tentacles, and white dragons were interruptive, disturbing even, and not something to dwell on. He found less and less that he drew the scenes from his memory. Indeed, the memory grew cold like a dinner plate left on the table too long.

Kyle would occasionally look out his window to Mr. Olsen's house on his way home. It would spark a memory that he once set out to walk the neighborhood and meet the man. But his dad would continue talking about Kyle's practice or the coming game and Kyle would look away. Look away. That was what he was doing, and what he continued to do... until the dragon showed up at the last football game.

CHAPTER 11

It was a Thursday evening. Lance and Kyle both got playtime in the last two games. The first game because their team was up by twenty-four points, and the second because they were down by thirty. Tonight was the final game of the season.

In the locker room before the game, their coach gave out superlatives. He told Kyle and Lance how proud he was of their effort. For two kids who never played and joined late, they were real contributors to the JV team and would be on varsity next year. They might even letter.

Kyle looked around at his teammates. He was so glad he joined the team. It gave him a new life, a new identity. He thought back to the day when Gwen suggested he try out. His worries were all so nerdy and dorky. Doppelgängers and dragons. Friday nights at a game shop with kids younger than him instead of in a stadium under the lights. Imaginings—

and he had come to believe that's what they were—about other worlds and missions with Merlin, the ancient wizard, were no more.

No, he had set aside that silly list for days of real enjoyment. He was a part of something now, part of a team. Maybe next year, a leader. He adjusted his shoulder pad as he looked around the field. It was raining but there was no thunder or lightning. A few kids complained, but the coach announced, "Only pansy sports stop because they get a little wet."

They warmed up, smelling like sweaty athletic gear and wet socks. Halfway through the first quarter the coach called Kyle off the bench to sub in. "Just 'till I talk to Joey. Couple of plays. Don't screw it up."

Kyle nodded feverishly, excited to go into a close game and in the first quarter. He jogged onto the field, taking his place as right-side linebacker. Their quarterback barked out his call. The ball snapped. The first play went to the other side. The play ended and Kyle returned to his position, waiting for the next snap. The quarterback shouted in a guttural voice, "Blue 42. 19. Hut! Hut!"

The ball snapped, and Kyle followed the handoff to the running back. The running back was headed for the tackle position right in front of Kyle. This was his play to fill the gap between the tackle and guard and make the tackle. He stepped up just as the running back pushed through the gap. Kyle wrapped him up.

He pounded his feet into the turf as he lifted up on the running back. Just like Wallace a weeks ago, Kyle felt the running back's feet leave the ground. The player stumbled backward. Kyle tackled him in the backfield. He looked up and the coach gave him a big thumbs up. Three plays later, Kyle returned to the bench. Lance came over immediately and slapped his helmet. "Way to go man!"

Kyle looked up in the stands. He wanted to see his dad there. He caught sight of his mom's bright pink umbrella and his dad in a yellow raincoat sitting next to her. His dad never liked umbrellas, always preferring the comfort of the raincoat or the drudgery of just being wet. While it was raining and a bit foggy, Kyle could tell his dad was smiling. He must have seen Kyle looking that way as he jumped up and gave Kyle a big wave.

Kyle started to give one back when suddenly, in the clouds behind the home stands, he saw the sky turning dark. There was a single spot in the sky darker than the rest, and it seemed to spread out, encompassing the light around it. It was as if the center section was devouring the very air as it grew. Then, Kyle saw it.

A long octopus-like tentacle swooped out of the dark center and through the air. It was half as long as the football field with what looked like un-popped zits all over it. Suction cups were on the underside of the tentacle, and each cup looked twice the size of Kyle. The tentacle had at least thirty of them! It swung through the air again and started a downward motion. Kyle heard several screams from behind him. No one on the home side could see it, but the visitor side had a front row view.

Lance slapped Kyle's helmet again. "Dude, you OK? You are looking off into—"

His comment ended as he looked up and saw what Kyle was staring at. The tentacle on its third sweep through the air descended, heading straight for the thirty-yard line where Kyle's teammates were standing. The tentacle struck, and there was an ear-popping thud. Dirt and turf flew everywhere. It looked like it missed Kyle's teammates, though several had been thrown to the ground by the impact. There was now a deep ravine from the thirty yard line to the forty.

The tentacle reared again, pausing twenty or so feet off the field. Its suction cups opened and closed as if it were... Kyle let the thought trail off. The tentacle reared back like a coiled snake before launching itself at the sideline. It wasn't just randomly there. It was looking for something... or someone.

The tentacle swept down where Kyle stood with the others on the sideline. He dove over a bench and rolled away just as the tentacle swiped at him. Looking up, he saw one of his teammates dragged onto the field. The tentacle raised him like one might examine a hair found on a dinner plate, then tossed him aside.

The boy fell ten feet or so to the ground. It looked as if his leg snapped on impact as he landed. Kyle scrambled to his feet, looking at the new tentacle-sized ditch stretching from the sideline to midfield. He couldn't help the sensation that this thing was not here to destroy haphazardly.

It was after him.

But why? *You know why,* he thought. *You look just like the boy that died in your backyard. Maybe you are that boy. And whatever that thing is, it doesn't want that boy or any version of him alive.*

Kyle looked up to try and see where the tentacle came from and what monstrous beast it was attached to. The tentacle seemed attached to empty space. If it had a torso it was lost in the fog. Or, as Kyle surmised, lost in another world.

Kyle unstrapped his helmet. He wiped the rain from his eyes with his arm. He also wiped the sweat from his forehead and squinted, following the appendage which grew in width and girth until it ended in the fog above the stadium lights. As the tentacle swung up and away, preparing for another downward swoop, the fog lifted momentarily.

What Kyle saw was space. Not space like empty sky, but space like of outer space. There was darkness with little speckles of light all around. Kyle couldn't be sure, but it looked like the body of whatever owned this tentacle was in that space. It was just sticking its arm, or tentacle, through a mousehole, swiping at whatever was in there. Or whoever. A very specific whoever, in fact.

The tentacle came crashing down again. It was Lance who saved Kyle from being squashed. Lance jerked Kyle's shoulder pad, pulling him a few feet to the left. "Dude!" was all he said, but it was enough. Kyle turned and ran.

He felt the ground heave up around him as the tentacle slashed at the field. A twenty-yard claw mark tore through the ground. Well, twenty-two to be exact. The field was marked off and measured after all. The turf and dirt lifted around the edges and Kyle was thrown onto his stomach.

He rolled over and saw the tentacle again swing upward and away. Everyone was rushing out of the stands. Most of his teammates had run off the field or were heading for the concrete bunker that was the locker rooms nearby. There was panic in the stands as people tried to escape, some even choosing to jump off the back of the bleachers or try and crawl under the small gaps to safety. Kyle looked but didn't see his parents or sister.

The tentacle crashed downward again. This time Kyle was alert and ran just out of its reach. However, now there was a trench on either side of him. There was no way Kyle and Lance could traverse the two ten-foot-deep ditches blocking their way. The only escape was a small undamaged section that led straight onto the field.

Kyle looked to the visitor side, which was similarly emptying out. Lance seized Kyle's shoulder pad again, and they locked eyes. It was just the two of them like it was back under that parking garage. In an instant, Kyle felt remorse. He felt like a fool that he let Gwen's flirting and the popularity of being an athlete interfere with the reality of the monster now attacking the field.

He and Lance were both guilty for not going to see Emory about the dragon they saw. But Kyle knew he was the guiltier party. He had seen this very monster in his own backyard and it had killed his doppelgänger.

I SAW HIM.

I HEARD HIM.

Now Kyle and his best friend were cornered like rats with only one way of escape. Unfortunately, the path out placed them both in the large open space where the tentacle could pick them off, but it was the only way. Without speaking, the two boys nodded agreement toward the only option available. Kyle and Lance ran.

Kyle resisted the urge to look behind him. He knew the tentacle was rearing for another swipe, and he couldn't outrun it. These would likely be his last steps, his last effort before being crushed. Or grabbed? Maybe the thing wanted him alive, wanted to take him into that other world. That would be worse than death. He had to look straight ahead and run as fast as he could.

In front of Lance and Kyle there was a bright flash of light that appeared over the stands. At first, Kyle thought he accidently looked into a stadium light, but it was too high and too bright.

Then he saw the source.

A white dragon swooped out of the clouds, flying just feet above his head. Kyle stopped running. In his peripheral, he saw Lance had stopped also. The dragon curved its path upward. A blast of white fire emitted from its mouth as it approached the tentacle. The appendage recoiled as the white colored flame made contact.

The dragon continued to soar toward the tentacle's point of origin. Just before impact, the dragon flipped its taloned feet in front of itself so its claws would strike first. The dragon's claws connected and locked onto the tentacle. It twisted and turned as it tried to pull away from the dragon.

About half its length disappeared into the dark area of the sky. Whatever creature thrust its arm in the hole now only wanted to pull it back out, to get away from the dragon. There was another flash of brilliant white light, and Kyle saw the dragon shoot another blast of its white fire. It released the tentacle from its grip, and the limb pulled back into the fog to whatever world it came from.

Everything went still. People stopped running as if someone pushed pause on a movie. Even Lance who stood next to Kyle stopped mid-step with a goofy look of panic and fear on his face. Kyle turned and saw the entire field was torn asunder. Several trenches ran across the grass under the stadium lights, making it look like small mountains had risen where there was once a flat football field.

The dragon swooped down and landed. It was eerie seeing a dragon in any moment of one's life, but in particular when the dragon seemingly pushed pause on the entire world. It and Kyle were the only two moving at all. Kyle looked again at the still forms.

One woman looked like she was in the middle of a sentence. A man was hovering in the air from his jump off the bleachers. It was bizarre to see him suspended in the air. There was no wind. No movement at all except for the dragon whose breath blew a frosty blast across

Kyle. He shivered. Lance, still frozen nearby, gave no indication he felt the bitter cold. He gave no indication he was capable of moving, even if he felt it.

The dragon spoke into Kyle's mind without a single movement of its lips. As before, it sounded both in his head and in shattering stereo all around him.

"Soon. You must go soon. Or this world too will be gone. He knows. He seeks all of you from all worlds. So few of you are left now. So few. He knows you are here and will come again. Find Merlin."

The dragon ascended. There was another flash of light, followed by a moment of stillness before the jumble of voices, screams, feet on stadium seating, and Lance catching his breath filled the air.

"Dude, that thing was like your drawings."

"Yeah, and that dragon was the same as the one we met," Kyle said, pointing to the now small figure flying away.

"Our dragon was here?!" Lance asked.

"Yeah, he saved us."

CHAPTER 12

The following week of school was canceled. FBI agents, specialists in weather phenomenon, avian experts, and what Kyle's dad called "Max Headrum's" flooded the small town with researchers, weather experts, news cameras, orange cones and yellow tape.

Several students and even a few parents had choppy cell phone videos of people bouncing around as they ran for cover. One senior cheerleader in particular had a video that showed the best image of the tentacle. It was blurry with a dust cloud that distorted the clarity. Despite that, it was clear something hit the field near the bleachers and sideline. The girl was touring America on news channels crying and sharing her story. Kyle's dad said she was also collecting some huge checks. Kyle saw her on her first interview.

She looked at the camera with tears in her eyes. "I don't know what it was. I just know I almost died."

In the privacy of his bedroom, Kyle couldn't help but hold an imaginary press conference where he told the world exactly what happened.

"So there is this monster from another world. It has come here to destroy our world. I know because a version of myself came to visit me. But don't worry, there is also a dragon that lives here. It came and protected us." He imagined everyone applauding and how famous he could be. He was no longer just an average bench-warmer football player, he was the headline for every news channel. No longer just somebody, he was the most important somebody on the planet as everyone listened to him tell the story.

But he did not tell anyone. No one would've believed him. No one knew what the thing was or how it happened, only that it was bizarre and otherworldly.

Kyle's parents were hesitant to let him or Libby outside for the first few days. Libby was fine with the new regiment of television and popsicles. Kyle couldn't stay still. His mind kept playing and replaying the dragon's words. "Soon. You must go soon. Or this world too will be gone. He knows. He seeks all of you from all worlds. So few of you left now. So few. He knows you are here and will come again. Find Merlin."

He pestered his mom to go outside. She put up a good resistance, but finally relented. Permission came with a lot of warnings. Stay in the yard. Stay near the house. If anything changes in the weather, come inside immediately.

Kyle hovered around the yard for an hour. He watched his mom periodically look out the window to check on him. First it was every few minutes, and then every five or ten. Then, finally, her check-ins ceased.

He went directly for Mr. Olsen's home.

Kyle cautiously opened the gate to the dilapidated fence and looked around. He made his way slowly to Olsen's front door. About half way there, something ran out from behind the house. Kyle jumped in surprise. He scanned the area in a moment of panic but didn't see anything.

There were a bunch of tall stones oddly placed in the yard. It reminded Kyle of pictures his class saw of old ruins where only parts of buildings remained. Except these weren't columns or brick walls. They were just really long stones and other stacks of rocks about ten feet high. A small patch of brownish-red fur scurried from one stack of stones to another in a flash. Its small eyes peered out from behind the rock, staring directly at Kyle.

Kyle took the next few steps to the front door slowly and with a great deal of caution. He looked around. The animal still had its gaze set on him, but it had not moved. Kyle turned his attention to the door. There was no doorbell. In its place there was a falcon, and its claws held a small cast-iron bell with a string hanging down. Kyle pulled the string left to right and the clapper hit the bell's sidewall.

He jumped back in surprise, not because of the bell's sound which was rather ordinary but because the falcon's wings flapped. It was then Kyle realized the falcon was not attached to the house wall. It flew up and around the home. As it did, the bell rang out. Kyle stepped back into the yard. He was spooked, but who wouldn't be. Sure, he had put on some muscle this football season, but he had a feeling muscle didn't matter in a yard where there was some sort of stalking critter and live gargoyle-like falcon doorbell.

Kyle decided it best to leave. He backed down the path, keeping one eye on the animal—was it a fox?—watching him, and another on the soaring falcon. Reaching the gate, he went to unlatch it. As he did, the falcon landed on the rail. It no longer had a bell in its talons. It now had a note. Kyle tried to reach for the gate handle but the bird pecked at his hand, then it raised the leg with the note. Kyle hesitantly leaned in to read the scribble.

Gone for emu feathers.

Mount Snowdon.

Don't feed the fox Boysenberries.

Kyle had no idea where Snowdon was. He only had the vaguest idea that Boysenberries was a type of jelly. He thought his dad bought some in the Smoky Mountains once. Whatever it was, he had no intentions of feeding anything to the fox. He had no intention of doing anything at all in this yard. The courage that helped him break away from his own yard against his mom's wishes was gone. The words of the white dragon took a backseat to Kyle's urgency for self-preservation.

The fox now lay on the path between Kyle and the house like a puppy tired out from playing. It gave a yawn, and the sound of a rooster came out. Kyle turned, reaching for the gate and hoping the falcon wouldn't do something to his hand, opened it, and ran into the street. Once there, he turned around. The falcon took flight back to the porch. The fox stood and gave another rooster sound before meandering back to the house itself. Kyle made for his own bedroom.

CHAPTER 13

It turned out that Snowdon was a real place. It was in Wales, which Kyle didn't know was part of England until he looked it up. The mountain was apparently a popular hiking destination, though Kyle couldn't imagine why someone as old as Mr. Olsen would want to hike up a really, really tall mountain. In the Wikipedia entry, there was also something about it being Rhita's tomb. Kyle didn't recognize her name from any of the books he read about Greek gods and he liked to think he had read all of the ones in his library.

Kyle also googled things like 'doorknobs that really are live birds,' 'foxes that sound like roosters,' 'emu feathers,' and 'Is Boysenberry bad for foxes?' All he found was that when a fox was mating, she might sound like a woman in distress. Kyle thought about times his mom was distressed or upset, but he couldn't remember her ever sounding like a rooster.

His attention shifted and instead, he began to look up what the thing was that came out of the sky at the football game. That was easier. And further, it gave Kyle a sense he was at least making progress. He felt in a weird spot. He now knew he couldn't ignore his doppelgänger's warning. It was confirmed by the dragon. One event Kyle might dismiss as boyhood imagination, but not multiple.

That said, there was a part of him that did not want to go see Mr. Olsen. Kyle once hung a hammock up in his back yard. He left it there and a few days later he went out to take it down. When he opened it up, a snake dropped out and slithered right over his shoe. It was a harmless garden snake, but he still ran from it. He did all sorts of things to avoid having to go take down the hammock after that experience. He felt the same way about Mr. Olsen's place.

Kyle knew the story of Perseus. He chopped the head off Medusa to use it to turn the kraken to stone. The kraken was a giant squid-like creature that lived in the deep sea. Kyle couldn't find any examples of a kraken in space, but it wasn't a far jump since space seemed like a vast ocean in some ways. The real question was *why* a kraken had torn up his football field. And on the last game, a game where he was getting to play.

Kyle thought he knew the answer. He just didn't want to admit it to himself. The doppelgänger in his back yard was real, and from somewhere else. Somewhen else? There was something from the space portal chasing the doppelgänger. Now, it might be chasing him. He knew there were things that existed in the world he never thought were possible, like a white dragon living underneath the mall parking garage. He had a feeling all of this was somehow about him.

Find Merlin.

He had tried. If Merle Olsen was Merlin, he wasn't home. He was off somewhere tracking down emu feathers. Weird.

Kyle closed up his laptop and put his brain on pause. Downstairs, his dad and mom were locked in on the television. They were showing the scene of the football field for the millionth time on the news. It was on local and national channels. Kyle even saw it on ESPN as the clip of the day. There was yellow police tape everywhere and scientists walking around in white lab coats.

"Everything tells us this was likely a tornado. They land, tear everything up, and then go away," said the scientist. The news reporter nodded feverishly, leaving the microphone in the scientist's face to continue. "How do you explain testimony—and I'm talking about eyewitness testimony here—that there was some sort of creature in the sky?"

The scientist cleared his throat. "There are several variations and testimonies don't wholly agree. I mean, it doesn't explain what people saw, but sometimes people think they see things. Sometimes even collectively they experience something so bizarre they don't have a category of explanation. Their mind makes them see something when they are trying to make sense of the chaos."

The reporter jerked the microphone back to himself. "But cameras don't do that. And we have footage of something in the sky. It certainly looks to me like it might be a tentacle as most eyewitnesses claim." He thrusted the microphone back to the scientist, almost hitting his chin.

The scientist frowned. "Well, this is the conundrum, is it not? Unfortunately, none of the videos are conclusive. For centuries, people have explained things they don't understand as mythical beasts. It is how we got the old Greek gods, sea monsters, even Big Foot. My scientific opinion is that whatever it was that caused the destruction that night was no more real than Big Foot or Zeus. The scientific community is still looking into everything. We just have to have an open mind about how science works and what may have happened."

Kyle's dad moved from his forward seated position to plop back against the couch. "What they need to do is keep their mind open about the possibility of an alien invasion."

"Now dear," Kyle's mom said as she glanced to make sure Libby wasn't in a panic, "Surely, you don't believe in—"

"What about the mall? The parking lot, I mean?" Kyle interjected over his mom's conversation. He looked at his dad who nodded slightly. "Some people there said they saw something flying away." Thinking he might have an ally, Kyle continued. "And there *was* something that night. Not only the monster, but a dragon. I was on the field. I know."

There. He said it. A weight lifted off him and he gave a louder sigh than he intended.

"A dragon!" Libby screamed. Her bottom lip quivered and she began to cry.

Kyle's mom gave him a glare only slightly less harsh than the one she gave to his dad. It was her "you better change the subject stare."

She went over to Libby. "They are just teasing. You know how boys are."

"Well, I know this," Kyle's dad said as he rose to his feet. He was excellent at taking cues from such stare-downs. "I know they are discussing evacuating the whole city if another incident happens. And I'm not going to leave this city before I have Momma's Pizza at least one more time. Who's up?"

Libby immediately jumped to her feet from her position playing on the floor. Her moment of fear traded in for a love of pizza and probably ice cream at the nearby Scoops. "Me! And can I get some pizza dough to play with?"

"Of course. Kyle?"

"Yes," Kyle said. He was less interested in Momma's trademark raw pizza dough for the kids to play with as he was getting a chance to get out of the house. "And dad, can Lance come with us? I mean, he's just a few streets away. He hasn't gotten to do anything since the Friday game. Like, nothing at all."

Kyle's dad nodded. "If his parents say it's OK. They are probably nervous like everyone else, but whatever it was that tore up that field could just as likely could strike here as Momma's Pizza."

Kyle's mom cleared her throat. Her eyes darted from Kyle's dad to Libby.

"I mean, unlikely to happen anywhere again, really. Certainly not anywhere near us. Tell you what, we'll see if the ice cream store is open, too."

Libby again transitioned from fear to joy.

Kyle boldly asked, "So dad, would you call Lance's mom or dad to ask? I mean, since everything is OK to go out and all."

Kyle's dad tilted his head, recognizing what Kyle just did. He'd used his words against him. He laughed and ran his hand through Kyle's hair as he walked by. "Sure, sure."

Everyone scattered to get ready. Kyle stayed near enough to listen in on his dad. He could hear his dad talking, and then long pauses as he listened to Lance's mom. In the end, she agreed. Kyle knew it not because of what his dad said, but because he heard Lance shout, "Yes! Awesome sauce!" so loud it came through his dad's phone.

A while later, they swung by Lance's house on the way to Market Street downtown where Momma's Pizza had stood for three generations. Momma was long gone, but the sign on the window promised to stay true to her recipes. Whether they did or not wasn't important. To Kyle and Lance, what was important was they got some good pizza and a chance to talk about that night on the field. And more importantly, their extraordinary luck.

At the other end of the restaurant, Emory was eating with a red-headed, freckled girl about his age. Apparently, the girl shared his love of pizza as they had two whole pizzas in front of them on the little raised pizza stands. Kyle figured they were on a date and that Emory probably didn't want to be disturbed. He also knew he might never get a chance to talk to Emory again, especially if the police made everyone evacuate the city. Kyle gave the excuse of checking out the pies at the front counter and made his way there with Lance, passing near Emory's table.

"Emory, it's me, Kyle," he loudly whispered as he drifted from the chocolate pie and coconut cake to Emory's spot near the window.

Lance was less subtle, talking so the whole restaurant could hear him. "Hey man! Yeah, we used to be at Epik Games like every Friday night."

The two boys stood awkwardly in front of the table for a moment. Kyle immediately thought this was a bad idea. Emory looked to be on a date. He probably didn't want to talk to high schoolers while he was with his girlfriend, especially not high schoolers who stopped hanging out with him because they became too cool and joined the football team. Kyle was wrong. Emory gave a huge smile.

"Yes, I remember you two. Of course. Faithful members 'till recently. Hate to have lost you."

"Well, we sort of joined the football team," Lance offered. "And they have games on Fridays."

The red-headed girl's eyes went wide. "Then you were there?" She leaned toward the boys expectantly.

"We were," Kyle said. He looked Emory in the eyes and leaned over their table, whispering, "And we saw your dragon."

"My dragon?" Emory quipped.

Kyle couldn't tell if Emory was brushing the conversation aside to avoid it in front of his girlfriend or if he was just humorously suggesting he didn't actually own a dragon.

Lance must've felt the same uncomfortable pause as he said in too loud a voice, "We mean, not *your* dragon. But like, the dragon you told us about."

Kyle looked between Emory and the girl to see if they had fumbled into ruining his dating life with nerdy dragon talk. Her eyes went wide, and she leaned even closer to Kyle and Lance. Kyle could smell her strawberry perfume.

"The one he saw as a kid! He told me all about it when that thing happened at the parking garage."

"And you believed him?" Kyle asked, wishing he could reach out and grab the words that escaped all too quickly.

"Of course." She reached around the two pizzas and held his hand. "Emory is a seer. He has the gift."

"It isn't that. Sometimes I just—"

"Sometimes he knows what is going on, like on a spiritual level or in a realm just out of reach for us. And sometimes he can see the things that are really hidden. That's what I love about him. Well, that and he doesn't believe pineapple should be on pizza."

"Is that why..." Kyle cleared his throat before continuing his impetuous question. "Is that why your eyes rolled back that night? Did you see something?"

Emory squeezed the girl's hand and looked at Kyle. His eyes rolled back, briefly flashing white. When his blue irises returned, Emory spoke. "I saw that your 'dream' wasn't so much as a dream as it was your reality."

"You knew I was... lying?"

"I knew you weren't ready to tell us the truth. And I understand. I, myself, only told you I saw that dragon once. In truth, I have seen it several times over the years. Flickers really, but enough to solidify it as real. That night it tore up the parking garage was the first time I ever saw it fly."

"Yeah, then and at the football field," Lance added.

"Oh, how I wish I could have seen that," Emory sighed. His girlfriend nodded vigorously. "Me, too."

"It was terrifying," Kyle said.

Emory nodded. "It probably saved your life. Or at least that is what I thought, reading between the lines of the news."

"Between the lines?" Lance asked.

"I mean, they didn't say it, but the info was there if you were looking."

Lance and Kyle nodded, but Kyle wasn't convinced. The news report seemed to deny any existence of an alien tentacle, a kraken, or a dragon. How could Emory listen to the same news stories Kyle had and think the reporters confirmed a dragon swooped in and saved everyone? Saved Kyle and Lance, in particular. Kyle started to ask Emory what he meant, but he stopped when he heard his name called from behind him.

It was his dad's voice. Their pizza was ready. "Hey," Kyle said, "we have to go. I just wanted to say… thanks, and sorry we haven't been there on Friday nights."

"It's OK," Emory replied.

His girlfriend interjected, "It is good you two are playing football. Emory agrees, don't you? He said it was a bummer you weren't coming on Friday nights anymore, but it was good you were building your strength. Emory also said— Ow!" She pulled her hand back after Emory squeezed it especially hard.

"Sorry Boze-bo, but it isn't our place."

"Place to what?" Kyle asked. He didn't know what 'Boze-bo' didn't say, but he wanted any help Emory could offer him.

The girl tossed her hair back and stared at Emory, then nodded her head in the direction of Kyle and Lance as if to say, "Tell them."

Emory didn't move.

"Tell them," she said more emphatically.

Emory motioned Kyle and Lance closer. The two boys leaned inward. His eyes rolled back.

It was just for a second, and his eyes flashed all white again. The pupils returned and he whispered, "You will need to leave soon. Very soon. I've seen the two paths. One, where you stay, leads to you and your families... well, it isn't good. And there are no rerolls if it goes that way. The other path is you travel. I don't know where. Seeing doesn't work that way. I just know you have to go. And soon. Or you will start losing the ones you love."

Kyle put a hand on the table to steady himself. He wanted to ask how Emory knew that, but he remembered his girlfriend called him a seer. In Dungeons and Dragons, that was someone who could see the future. Kyle was about to say something when he was interrupted again by his dad's voice. This time, it was much more agitated.

"We're waiting, Kyle. You know we won't eat until we pray."

His mom chimed in, too. "Until *all* of us pray."

Kyle felt a lump in his throat. He looked at Emory. He had so many questions, but there was no time, so he managed a weak, "OK." It seemed inadequate.

He turned back to his family and rejoined their table. Libby offered a fast prayer. "God, thanks for the food. Help everyone everywhere. Especially people who don't have pizza to eat. Amen."

Kyle kept his eyes shut a moment longer. He just needed a moment to clear his head. When he opened them, his dad and Libby were already holding a slice of pizza. Libby's cheese was sliding off the crust, and his mom was forking a bite of salad into her mouth. Did his decision to find Merlin mean he would have to leave? And if he didn't find Merlin, did that mean his parents and sister would die? He heard the words of his doppelgänger within his mind:

Just listen. My time is short. Not from the future. A different world. They are coming. In my world, they are already here.

He picked up a slice of pepperoni, not realizing it was the last meal he would eat on his own world.

CHAPTER 14

Kyle's family, along with Lance, exited Momma's Pizza. Kyle and Lance waved goodbye to Emory and his girlfriend as they walked outside. The only parking spot when they arrived earlier was street parking two blocks down. Enjoying their walk, Libby asked if she could get some ice cream at Scoops, a local creamery between Momma's Pizza and the car. Kyle's dad agreed.

"OK, but your dad spoils you, I swear," his mom said. "I'll take you in. If he does, you'll both come out with three scoops each." She shot him a smile that said she loved him but he'd be the one up dealing with her sugar rush after bedtime.

"Or a chocolate milkshake! Extra large!" Libby shouted. "With sprinkles and cookie bits!" She swung the door open to the shop and was inside before Kyle's mom could even catch the door.

In a rush to prevent chocolate overload, his mom rushed to the counter to head off her child's order. As the door was closing, Kyle heard her say, "No you will—"

Kyle did a doubletake. His mom was frozen in the store. Her foot was hovering as if she took half a step before someone immortalized her in statue form. Libby was frozen in time, too. Her feet were off the ground mid-jump as she tried to look into the glass case to see the flavors. The door remained partially opened, as if an invisible hand was preventing it from closing.

Kyle spun and saw his dad's face was petrified with an expression of laughter, enjoying the moment between his wife and daughter. Lance had his gaze set across the street where three college girls were walking. The one in a yellow sundress was in the middle of her own sentence as she stood stock still, pointing up to the Chattanooga Choo-Choo sign. All the cars on the road were stopped, but there were no squeals of brakes or visible accidents.

Everything was frozen. Everything and everyone except for Kyle. He moved his hands in front of his face as evidence, and even lifted a foot off the ground and moved it a step away.

Nothing else moved. Everything was immobile except for him. Well, everything but him and a white cloud moving in over the downtown street… and the white dragon emerging from the cloud.

The dragon flew down into an open area of the road. As he landed, Kyle heard an audible "whoosh" followed by a snorting sound as the dragon inhaled sharply. A cold blast of wind encircled the whole block, giving Kyle a chill.

"I can… you can… I mean can I…" Kyle stumbled to put a sentence together.

The answer to his unasked question came both inside Kyle's head and in stereo all around him. "We must talk."

"How are you doing this?" Kyle pointed at his mother midway through the door to Scoops, then to a car stopped under the nearest traffic light. "How are they frozen? It's just like at the game." The words slowly caught up with his spinning brain.

"They are not dead. Nor are they frozen. Indeed, they still move, just at such a slow rate it appears as if they don't. Come. We must speak."

What the dragon meant was it would speak, and Kyle would listen.

"How do you say… the kraken? Yes, that is right. The kraken. It knows you are here, and it will not stop searching for you. Even if I am able to defeat it, another will come, if not other things much more terrifying. He has many allies, and the kraken is but one of them. Your family, your world, will die. You must go find Merlin and begin your journey. As long as you remain, your world is in danger. If you don't go, all worlds will be in danger."

"Why me?" Kyle stepped off the curb. As he did, it became even more difficult to see the dragon eye to eye. Even bulked up from playing football, Kyle was still tiny compared to this majestic creature. "Why do I have to go?"

"You are one of them. There are very few of you left, and he is looking for all of you. At this point, you may be the only one that remains. I do not know for certain. Rumors spread, and so many others have died."

"What does that even mean? That guy in my backyard—"

"That was you from another world. The world you must go to."

"Well, he had his intestines ripped out and he died. He bled out in my back yard. I don't really want to go through that. He was so strong and powerful. I'm nothing like him. I mean, whatever did that to him would kill me quick."

"Still, you must go."

"Why?" Kyle held his arms up as he pointed at himself. "My doppelgänger even said I wasn't important."

And there it was. Kyle had not been bullied, nor was he a bully. He was invisible. He wasn't the star athlete; he was just a kid on the bench. A substitute. He was neither a valedictorian nor the kid failing his classes. He was not an artist, an actor, or anything else. He could go missing and the world would continue as is without interruption.

Sure, his parents would miss him, but they had Libby, the spoiled younger child. Lance would miss him, but Lance too was like Kyle. Just average. Neither of them were the guys you called to step up and lead. They were the kids who sat in the middle of classrooms, the ones the teacher never disciplined and never called on. They weren't expected to participate. Just fill the room, like a human moat between the bad kids and the good kids.

What the dragon was asking required Kyle to take initiative, to lead. Kyle had never taken the lead. Even joining the football team wasn't his idea. He did it because a pretty girl suggested it. It didn't scare him as much as it just seemed so distant of a thought, like when his geography teacher talked about what they needed to know if they ever went to Europe. It was so far away, and such an impossibility, Kyle couldn't see a reason to engage. Yet this dragon had frozen the whole block, maybe even the whole city, to talk with him. Why?

"Aithusa? Aithusa? Aithusa!!"

The voice startled Kyle who instinctually jumped back onto the sidewalk. He spun his head side to side trying to identify the voice. Emory came running down the street. Well, more like jogging slowly. He was moving. Emory was moving! Someone other than Kyle and the dragon was able to move.

"Aithusa! It is you. Like, really you." Emory tossed his half-eaten pizza slice to the street and wiped his tomato stained mouth with his sleeve. "I can't believe you are really here. I told my girl, but something is wrong. She..." his words drifted off as he saw Kyle's family frozen in place along with the three college girls and a handful of cars. "What's happening? Why are they still and I'm not?"

"Ah, the seer. Thank you, sir. You have done well training this boy."

"Training?" Kyle and Emory said in unison.

"Yes. In this world one cannot learn on the battlefield nor in actual places of utter despair, broken dreams, or forgotten hopes. It is unfortunate. Yet, you have taught him strategy and cunning in so far as you could."

"You mean our D&D games?" Kyle asked. "I mean, no offense to Emory, but like, they are just games."

"NO!"

The dragon rose up, and a wind so cold that even with his jacket on Kyle felt like he was in a walk-in freezer in a T-shirt. He couldn't imagine how Emory felt, who ran out of the pizza place in cargo shorts and a tee.

The dragon's feet came back to the ground, and cracks spiderwebbed from where they touched, creating a ditch that stretched to the other side of the three-lane road. "Listen. This world is not important. But you are. You must go take your place in the lynchpin world."

Emory lifted his arms and pretended to put something invisible into his left hand. Kyle realized Emory was miming what a lynchpin did. It was as if he was inserting something small into an invisible machine.

"A lynchpin, like this."

"Lynchpin? The guy who looked like me and died in my back yard used that word." Kyle shivered, unsure if it was the cold or the memory of his doppelgänger.

"Lynchpin. It is like a metal pin that holds a wheel on an axle. Is that right, Aithusa?"

"Well spoken, seer." The dragon looked at Kyle. "You are correct. The one who died is the "Kyle" of the lynchpin world. You must go and take his place. If that world falls to darkness, so too does everywhere else that exists. Guard your trust in others and do not believe everything you hear. You are of grand importance, much more than I or an Aithusa."

"Are you… or like versions of you, in other worlds too?"

"No. No one is in every world, not even Kyle Pendragon. Yet in some there are likely to be kindred souls to myself. We are forever bound to the world we are spawned in, but in the scheme, we are unimportant."

"How can you say a dragon that can freeze time and battle an alien kraken is unimportant?!"

Kyle saw in his peripheral Emory was nodding. At least Emory saw his point.

The dragon didn't exactly laugh, but it was close. A plume of smoke drifted from her nostril. "On this world I may be unique, but on many I am commonplace. On others, my kind is extinct. I can only travel within my own world, but I know these things because I listen. I listen to the ones who walk the planes, to those who tell the tales."

"But I'm not a planeswalker. How do I get there? Will you not come with me?"

"Find Merlin. And soon. He alone here on this world is a planeswalker. I must go now before my hold weakens."

Emory stepped down from the curb and wrapped his arms around the dragon's neck. Tears were rolling down his cheek. "I knew you were real. I knew it. Thank you for letting me… letting me come out here and not be… not be frozen." He ended the hug and stepped back up onto the curb.

"You are a seer. Such magic will never work on you. And it is I and Kyle who thank you for your service to him. It will serve him well on his quest."

Emory stuttered. "C-can my Boze-bo… can she maybe see you?"

The dragon snorted a reply. A moment passed in silence, then Emory's girlfriend rushed out of Momma's Pizza, gasping. "Emory! It's true! Emory, I see him, too!"

Emory wiped a tear from his cheek before telling the dragon, "Thank you."

Kyle got the notion to do the same. He started to ask if his family could see her, and Lance, too, but there was no opportunity. The dragon lifted into the air. Seconds later, she disappeared inside the white cloud. Everyone was free of the time stop.

"Oh! I'm so sorry. I wasn't looking," Lance said as he tumbled right into Emory. "Hey, wait. Emory? You weren't out here. And Kyle, you were, like, over there? What's going on?"

"What's going on?" Emory said with a big grin. "You ever have the thought that you just aren't important? Like, maybe not a loser, but just not important? And then a dragon comes and tells you that you're a seer?" He put an arm around Kyle and gave him a quick hug. "Kyle, do what he said." Emory turned to his girlfriend who was running down the street. "Oh, Boze-bo! Can you believe it?!"

CHAPTER 15

The next day at school, Lance and Kyle went over all the details of the previous night for the tenth or eleventh time. They both landed themselves an afternoon of detention for disruption in Mrs. Wileman's class, but it wouldn't be served for another week, so it did little to squelch their conversation in any other class they shared.

The only thing that pulled them away was Kyle's newest drawing. He couldn't sleep and woke up at five with a clear vision. The drawing was almost lifelike. This one had the squid in it again. Kyle was almost certain now that the tentacle was attached to a space squid of some kind. A kraken.

It had Kyle and Lance in it, too. And no matter how much Kyle tried not to draw it, the picture had his sister laid out on the ground as if she were dead. In a moment of clarity, he scribbled some raindrops on the page.

"Is it raining when this happens?" Lance asked somberly.

"Yes, I think so. That's how I see it, anyway."

"It is about to rain right now." They both looked outside the window at the incoming storm. Mrs. Langston coughed her "pay attention" cough and Kyle tucked the drawing up under his worksheet.

By the time Lance and Kyle were on the bus, the overcast sky had turned into heavy rain and wind. The bus was humid inside with all the windows up. It smelled like gym socks and BO with a slight hint of cheap tween girl perfume. Kyle couldn't wait until he was sixteen and didn't have to ride the bus home anymore. He also couldn't wait util this particular bus ride was over, hopefully without any incidents.

He closed his eyes and imaged being in his dad's old truck, pulling out in front of the bus. He had his sister and Lance in the front bench seat with him. His sister. Kyle opened his eyes and looked around for Libby. As he did, everything started to spin. He felt dizzy, and his stomach threatened to send up all the cafeteria chicken nuggets he had eaten for lunch.

He couldn't get his bearings and found himself losing track of what was going on around him. The humid air and continual bounce of the bus caused the nausea to increase. The air twisted around him. There was a jolt, a sharp pain in his shoulder, then another jolt. The world went into chaos around him. He closed his eyes and tried to breathe deeply.

Kyle felt a warm ray of light on his face. He also felt Lance land on him. He opened his eyes to see his window below him. The bus was sideways on the asphalt road. The world spun again as the bus rolled. He grabbed onto a leg of the bench seat and gained enough awareness to understand he and Lance were jammed under their seat, which kept them from going into freefall. There were screams and shouts of those not so lucky. Another tumble and the bus came to a stop on its side in a ditch. There were no seatbelts, so everyone had been tossed around like socks in a dryer.

Lance put his elbow into Kyle's side in an effort to stand up. Kyle moaned and stood himself. He could feel he would have many more bruises than Lance's elbow. The girl in the aisle across from them was hanging on to her seat, trying not to fall on Kyle and Lance.

Kyle reached up and caught her, helping to ease her down. The bus driver's head was drooping against the window. He looked to be unconscious, maybe even dead.

Libby screamed from the back of the bus. Kyle looked and saw flames coming out of the floorboard. He glanced around in panic. There were no adults here other than the driver. Kyle shouted, "The rear exit! The bar, lift it up. Lift it up!"

A kid in Libby's grade tentatively pushed on the bar.

"You have to shove it hard! Push it up!" Kyle said.

Libby joined the boy and together they raised the bar. It didn't really push upward as much as to the left due to the bus being sideways in the ditch, but they understood, and the door flopped open. Students began exiting out of the back. There were only five or so back there, as the bus had already made half its stops.

Kyle and Lance moved to the front with the girl across from them. She climbed out of the door, which now served as the roof of the bus, and stood there a moment, watching flames come out of the windows in the back. She carefully maneuvered to the side where the embankment was steepest and jumped down before climbing up the ditch to the roadside. The girl joined the other students on the side of the road.

"We have to go," Lance said.

Kyle nodded his head toward the driver. There was a *pop* as several seats caught fire. "We have to help get him out."

Lance helped Kyle try and wake up the driver. He mumbled something incoherent, but did not try to unbuckle. At least he was alive. The flames started getting closer. Kyle knew they had to move soon. Lance tugged on Kyle's arm, "We got to go, man. Like, now."

"Then help me." Kyle unbuckled the driver and the rest of his body flopped downward. He tried to pull on the driver's arm, but he was too heavy.

"Like, we gotta go now," Lance repeated.

Kyle gave one last try. He put his arms underneath the armpits of the driver and let out a groan. A groan wasn't the right word. It was more like a deep growl. The kind of growl he would expect a bear to make before it attacked. Certainly, it was not the kind of sound he expected to hear come from his own mouth.

To his amazement, the man grew lighter. Kyle felt a surge of power. Without strain, Kyle lifted the bus driver over his own head. It wasn't done in ease, but it was far easier than it should have been. It felt similar to the surge of energy and power he had experienced the day he flipped Wallace. Kyle stood there, holding the driver above his head. He found a foothold on a nearby seat and lifted. The driver's body now was outside the bus, but he couldn't reach quite high enough to lay him down safely.

Lance crawled up through the opening, squeezing past the driver, then stood on the atop bus and grabbed the driver's arms and pulled with enough effort that Kyle was able to move from the man's armpits to his waist and then push up on his feet. Kyle gave another growl and shoved the driver up and out. The driver's belly drug across the stop sign that always flapped out when the bus let off passengers.

Kyle used the rail bar to climb out himself. As he exited, he felt the heat from the fire inside. The bus driver woke and screamed. "Tentacles! What the—" He flailed his hands as if he was still driving. He likely would have fallen back into the bus if the stop sign had not caught on his belt.

Kyle and Lance waited until the driver calmed down, then they helped him untangle his belt and the three jumped onto the embankment as the girl had done. There they scrambled away from the burning bus. Once on the road, the bus driver looked around. "Where are the other kids?"

"They went out the back door. They are over there." Lance pointed a short distance down the road where a group of kids huddled in the rain.

"It isn't safe. There's a... a hole," the driver said more to himself than to the boys. "The earth just opened up in front of us. All I could do was swerve. I hope I didn't hurt anyone. Oh, I'll be fired for this for sure! But it wasn't my fault. The earth just opened up."

"Like an earthquake?" Lance asked. He wiped his rain-soaked face in order to look out at the road. Kyle did the same.

"Like a crack. But there was... man, I can't even... I swear I saw a large tentacle, like an octopus, but floating in the sky. It came down so fast..."

"And it made a hole in front of the bus?" Kyle offered.

The driver nodded, unable to add anything to Kyle's spot-on description.

Kyle looked around for the tentacle. What he saw terrified him. There was a long ditch like the night on the football field. Except this time, the tentacle had torn through asphalt and concrete rather than soft dirt. It seemed the tentacle could cut through just about anything. Kyle's hand moved to his own stomach as he remembered his disemboweled doppelgänger.

Up in the sky, the air was glistening. It was almost like the shimmer of his sister's glitter hairspray. And just as her glitter would shuffle off and go everywhere, the shiny area seemed to shift and move as well. Kyle thought the best explanation was that the air became wavy, like in a TV show when there is a dream sequence and the screen folds and moves to tell you what you are about to see wasn't real.

Kyle knew what he saw was all too real. In the center of the thin, wavy sky there was a blurred space. Not quite a fog or a mist, but like looking through a dirty glass door. Or like looking through glasses when they steam up just enough to make everything still visible but blurry. You could see everything on the other side, but it was somehow separate from where you were. And on that other side was not just a tentacle, but the entire kraken. And the hole was growing big enough for it to enter completely.

The rain was coming down hard. Steam drifted up off the roadway. It was thickest near the road's center yellow line. It was there that Kyle saw the large tentacle strike again. It lifted from the ground and swung to the bus, striking it. It seemed indifferent to the fact the bus was now completely engulfed in fire. The tentacle effortlessly lifted the bus upwards.

Kyle turned his head to see the driver running away as fast as he could. He called for Lance and Kyle to follow him. As they started toward him, another tentacle swung low and snagged the driver. It held him in its grip and squeezed.

The man's head expanded like a balloon, and Kyle expected to see the driver's eyes bulge out from the pressure being exerted like in a cartoon. Instead, the driver went limp and was dropped to the ground. His head still looked a bit oversized for his body and there were suction marks all along his back where the tentacle had grabbed him.

Kyle and Lance looked at each other in sheer panic. The tentacle holding the flaming bus tossed the vehicle toward the other kids, toward Kyle's little sister. He screamed, "Libby! Get away! Get away! Run!" He knew even as he did it there was no way she would hear him.

Kyle shouted a guttural "No!" from his throat as he watched the bus's trajectory. It was going to land right on top of his sister and the other kids. They started to scatter but had no chance of avoiding the vehicle.

The bus stopped. Well, it didn't stop, but it slowed, and the fire turned to steam. The head of a white dragon rose above the bus. It flapped its wings, but one of them was injured. Kyle could see it did not have the same range of motion as the other. Aithusa looked toward the sky and let out a breath of ice and frost wind.

Up in the air, Kyle saw the entirety of the kraken was now on his side of the portal. Its tentacles all rose from their various places of destruction and pointed toward the dragon, the appendages spreading outward to form a cone shape. The blast of ice from Aithusa's breath shattered. The tentacles that had been frozen by the ice came back to life. If the dragon couldn't stop it, what could? And what other evil might it be capable of doing? The answer came all too soon.

From the kraken's underbelly shot an oozing, green slime. Aithusa rose and spread her wings. The majority of the green ooze hit the dragon's chest and outstretched wings. Kyle watched with horror as some of the ooze soared past Aithusa towards the kids from the bus. Towards Libby. Kyle saw the scene with a clarity that seemed impossible when one considered the speed at which it happened.

The ooze splashed against the hillside where the kids huddled together. A little girl screamed for her mommy. She must have been in kindergarten or first grade judging by how small as she was. As the green liquid rushed toward the girl, Libby stepped in front of her, blocking the girl with her body. The splatter landed on Libby's back. Kyle watched helplessly, too far away to do anything. Two other kids were covered in the ooze, and they dropped to the ground, lifeless. The girl in Libby's embrace yelled again for her mother before reaching out to touch Libby. When she did, Libby too fell lifelessly to the ground.

The dragon landed on the ground with a thud. Her head bowed down as if in pain. The kraken's tentacles began swinging again. Kyle noticed there were numerous cars around him with open doors. Some people were running off the road while others ran toward the children. A tentacle swiped a light pole. The transformer blew and sparks erupted. Another tentacle struck through a car window, lifting the vehicle in the air before tossing it aside. Kyle hoped its driver had already fled.

Then everything went still. Everything but the kraken, Aithusa, and himself.

The dragon sprang upward and into the kraken's midsection. A blast of ice came from its mouth as its claws made contact. Tentacles searching for targets on the ground twisted upward and wrapped around the dragon. Aithusa began to squirm and fight as the kraken squeezed her. Kyle knew there was no one who could help. Even if the US military had a fighter plane or a tank, it wouldn't come. The dragon had slowed the world and no one could help her.

No one but Kyle.

But what could he possibly do? He was nobody. Insignificant even among other boys. Less so among dragons and mythical beasts. He couldn't exactly fly up into the air where the two were fighting. There was no way he could reach the kraken.

Except...

There was one tentacle hanging limply. It seemed unable to join the others as the beast fought Aithusa. It dangled down from the kraken's body, the tip lying flat on the road with a sword stuck into it. It wasn't just any sword. It was his doppelgänger's sword.

Kyle ran. He saw Aithusa break free only to have one of her legs wrapped by a tentacle. She flapped her wings to escape, but the tentacle around her leg pulled her back down. Another tentacle swung up and landed on top of her, smashing her to the ground. The kraken's other appendages reared back for another strike.

In the sky, Kyle saw the kraken emerge further from the portal. It was descending rapidly to finish its prey. Kyle ran to the sword. He skidded to a halt and grabbed onto the hilt, pulling with all of his might.

It didn't budge. He tried again as Aithusa let out a breath of frost in the kraken's face. The dragon was clearly weakened, her breath nothing like what Kyle saw moments ago. He pulled again. Nothing. He issued that roar, the one he found while in the bus. Or maybe he had found it that day with Wallace. Now it was louder. He let it come out as it wanted.

"Roar!"

The blade slid free. Kyle wielded it in both hands. While it was heavy, its weight was perfectly balanced. He swung it left to right and up and down without resistance. It was as if it was an extension of his arm, a very lethal extension. Kyle couldn't determine in the few seconds between picking up the blade and wielding it whether it was his own inner strength that made the task so easy or if the blade itself was somehow helping him. Either way, it was a conundrum that the blade both felt immensely heavy and extremely light at the same time. It was as if he could barely lift it while at the same time he felt as if he could swing it all day without tiring.

Kyle held the sword over his head as he ran toward the kraken. With Aithusa on the ground being pommeled by tentacles, the kraken had descended within reach. Kyle jumped and swung, piercing a portion of the kraken's lower body just above one of its tentacles. The blade buried deep into its flesh, shifting a bit under Kyle's weight but staying lodged within the beast. The kraken gave a high-pitched scream, and all of its tentacles extended outward and flapped as if trying to fly.

The kraken began to ascend while it continued to scream. Kyle realized he was still holding onto the hilt of the sword. He had to let go before he got too high into the air. If that happened, he would either fall to his death or go with the kraken to whatever was behind that shiny, wavy portal. He let go and tumbled to the ground.

The kraken quickly fled through the portal. The scream continued until the kraken's head disappeared into the blackness, then it faded.

Kyle ran to Aithusa. He noticed everything was no longer frozen, but things weren't moving normally, either. "Are you okay? I thought..." Kyle didn't know what to say and he let the statement hang in the air.

The dragon's voice came slow and labored. "That was a good strike. Perhaps even lethal, Kyle, son of Pendragon."

"Are you... are you okay?"

"Paralysis is setting in. Do not touch me nor anyone stricken. All those hit by the kraken's..." Aithusa paused. Kyle saw the dragon's head sag as it struggled to continue speaking.

"What can I do? Is there something that reverses it?"

"Yes, but not here. Find Merlin. Quickly, before the kraken or another denizen returns. There are many under his command now." The voice became frail and weak. Kyle could no longer hear the dragon externally, only a diminishing voice inside his own head. Aithusa was dying.

He heard a scream as someone nearby realized there was a dragon. Everyone was returning to full motion. Kyle had to concentrate to hear Aithusa's final words. "You... must... find... Merlin."

Aithusa collapsed on the roadway.

Kyle put his hand out to touch the magnificent creature, then pulled it back so as not to touch any part covered in the kraken goo. He could see her neck pulsing in and out, but it was slowing, unlike the world around him that was now in a panicked terror. Aithusa's hold on time slipped and chaos erupted.

"I will," Kyle said. He took a few steps back, careful not to touch any of the kraken's spray.

CHAPTER 16

Kyle's attention turned to Lance as his friend called his name. "Kyle! Your sister!"

He spun and saw Lance running toward Libby who lay face down on the ground. Kyle screamed. "Stop! Stop! Don't touch her! Lance! Don't touch her!"

Lance stopped, surprised by the command in Kyle's tone. "We have to. If she's alive and face down, she'll suffocate."

"No!" Kyle's single word came out with a deep, resonating growl behind it. It was enough. Lance stopped. Kyle took three careful steps forward and placed his hand on Lance's shoulder, and the two backed up, never taking their eyes off the scene.

"Just trying to help, man."

"I know. You can't touch that stuff. I don't think you can even touch anyone who has touched it." Kyle pointed to the green ooze scattered around the ground and on his sister.

As if to punctuate Kyle's warning, one of Libby's friends ran up to her prone body. Before Kyle could warn her, she knelt and put her hand on Libby's arm.

"Libby! Are you… O.M.G, so gross." The girl lifted her hand and examined the green goo, then slung her hand down and a glob slid off her fingers to the ground. "That is so—" She never got to finish the sentence. Instead, she fell to the ground with a thud.

"That stuff, it paralyzes," Kyle said, hoping Lance would believe him without experimenting.

"How do you know that?" Lance asked.

"The dragon told me."

Kyle waited for Lance to tell him he was crazy, but no such judgement came. He supposed it was easier to believe in dragons when one was literally ten yards away. The two took a moment to look around. As people rushed to the scene, those who came in contact with the substance began to collapse. It seemed there was no end to the terror.

Kyle watched as someone reached to assist a limp body twenty yards away from where the ooze had splashed. It seemed impossible the person had come in direct contact with the kraken spray, yet the one who touched the body fell limp and lifeless. Where several students and a dragon once laid, there was now a pile of twenty or so people.

"Come on," Kyle said. "We can't help her or Aithusa here. We have to go."

Lance nodded and the two took pains to walk away, avoiding stray patches of ooze and infected bodies. An ambulance door opened nearby and a paramedic hopped out of the unit. Kyle heard him mutter, "Oh, my Lord." He began walking toward Kyle and Lance. The driver joined him.

"You two okay?" he asked as he approached.

"Yes," Kyle said.

"OK. Stay right here out of the way. God awful shame you young kids have to see—what the hell? Sarah! Look! It wasn't a joke. There's a dragon." He pointed at the beast in the road with several paralyzed bodies around her.

"Sir," Kyle said. The two started walking toward the dragon. "Sir." Further still they walked. "Sir!" Kyle's voice grew in strength. The man continued ahead, focused on the scene. The woman turned.

"Yes?"

"Ma'am, the dragon. It saved everyone here. It may not look like it but—"

"All I see are a bunch of people lying dead or wounded around it," she said. She started to turn back to follow her partner.

"Ma'am!" Kyle was yelling now. She turned around, giving him a glare that said all too well he was interrupting her from her real work. "Ma'am, there was something in the sky. A kraken, I think." She placed a hand on her hip. Naming a mythical creature probably lost him credibility rather than gained it, but Kyle continued before she could stop him. "That goo and ooze came from it. Don't touch it. Anyone who does will be paralyzed."

"Paralyzed? Right. You two stay out of the way." She spun dismissively and jogged a few steps to catch up with her partner. He arrived at the first fallen victim and Kyle watched with horror as the paramedic lifted up the person's body. In seconds, he too collapsed.

The female paramedic stopped cold in her tracks. She turned to the boys. "What did you say again?"

Kyle stepped toward her and gave her the short version of the story, leaving out the part where he seized a sword from another world and plunged it into the kraken, driving it back into a space portal.

"So anyone who touches them…" she looked over and saw a man running from his truck. He wore a pair of khakis and a golf shirt. A business man on his way somewhere when he saw the chaos and jumped out to help. He ran to the nearest body on the ground and touched the person's arm. A few seconds later he, too, was laying on the ground motionless.

"What the hell…?" the woman said.

"You have to get people to stop going up and touching everyone," Lance told her.

The woman nodded and clicked the radio speaker hooked to her shoulder. "This is Sara with the county EMS. I need all police officers to put up a perimeter immediately. Treat the situation like an active chemical spill. And do not touch the bodies. Repeat. Do not touch the bodies."

She repeated the request several times and looked over to the two boys. They were gone.

CHAPTER 17

Kyle and Lance ran toward Kyle's subdivision. It was only a few blocks away from where the bus overturned. Still, the sprint winded both boys. The entry road split after the first few homes. One way led to Kyle's house, and he needed to tell his parents about Libby and let them know she was OK. The other road led to Merle Olsen's place, and he needed to "Find Merlin."

Kyle pulled his phone out and tapped his mom's number. The phone showed a little spinning circle followed by a notice that all networks were busy. Lance was getting the same message.

"I'm sure everyone is trying to use their phones right now. It happened to me once when my family went to a concert. My dad said we must've 'overloaded the tower' or something like that."

Lance timidly asked, "Man, shouldn't we go to your house? Get your parents? Call mine.

You got a home phone, right? My mom will be worried."

"If I go home, I'll have to stay there."

"Yeah, I can too, if you don't mind. At least 'till—"

"I can't stay." Kyle turned to Lance. "If you want, you can go to my house. Here," Kyle unsnapped a carabiner with a key dangling on it from his backpack and held it out to Lance. "You can go inside. Call your parents on our home phone. And tell my parents... tell them..."

Kyle paused. Tell them what? His sister was paralyzed and maybe dead because a giant space kraken spewed ooze at her? And not only that, but if he had listened to his dying doppelgänger or the dragon none of this would've happened. Now, their son needed to travel to who knew how many worlds where he would likely be eviscerated and die.

Kyle looked again at the road to his house and the one to Merle Olsen. He made his decision. If he went home, he would do nothing. The police would evacuate the city, and he wouldn't even get to see Olsen. More krakens would come without a dragon to help them. Kyle looked at Lance.

"Just tell them I love them." He extended the carabiner.

Lance didn't take the key. "Where are you going?" He gazed over Kyle's shoulder to Mr. Olsen's yard, and Kyle knew his friend already knew the answer.

"Don't you get it, Lance? All of this is because of that guy in my yard. If I don't do what he says, more stuff will come. This time it got my sister. I hope she's OK, but who knows? And next time, it might be my mom or dad. Or you. Or maybe even this whole city. This whole world, even. If that thing is really after me, then I have to go talk to this guy. Maybe he isn't Merlin, but maybe he is. That night with the fox and the weird falcon doorknob certainly made it seem like he might be magical or something."

"You think there is a wizard in your neighborhood and no one knows?" Lance continued to stare over Kyle's shoulder at Olsen's yard.

"A few months ago, I would've said, 'No,' but I also didn't think there was a dragon living under the mall parking garage, either."

"OK," Lance said. It was enough for Kyle. He didn't ask if Lance still wanted the keys.

Instead, he reattached them to his backpack and the two walked toward Olsen's home.

Olsen's yard was partitioned off by a privacy fence on the sides and an old rusty chain-link fence that ran along the front yard facing the street. Most of the chain-link fences he'd seen were four or five feet tall, but this one was easily twice his height and had barbed wire on top of it.

Kyle couldn't recall if it was that high on his first visit or not. Perhaps it was and he just didn't notice, but he also suspected that the fence may have grown a bit. It certainly wouldn't be the strangest thing he'd seen recently. The gate was surrounded by two columns of stone that sat on the sidewalk and there was no visible watchguard. There was now a padlock on the latch. Kyle jiggled it uselessly. The gate was locked.

"What now?" Lance asked.

"Weird. It was unlocked the other night."

Kyle stepped back onto the street. On the side yard near the McCorkle's pool there was a crushed section of fence with a rotting tree resting on top. Someone had cut the tree a few feet from the road, but the trunk in Olsen's yard and the portion on the fence was never removed.

"Maybe we can get in there," Kyle said, pointing.

"I don't know. It's one thing to go through the gate and knock on his door. It's another to climb a fence. What if he sees us and thinks we are breaking in?"

"We are," Kyle acknowledged. "And if he isn't the one we—I—am supposed to see, then he is already going to freak out. Two kids showing up in his yard talking about other universes and large squids eating busses... jumping his fence will be the least of his worries." Kyle gave his best reassuring smile to Lance, though he knew it was forced. "The other night, that falcon was like a doorknob. And it went from his porch to the gate and held out a note. That isn't normal either. Maybe not squid and dragon fighting weird, but enough to tell me he might be the one."

Lance nodded. The two boys climbed onto the rotting tree and slid down its length. As they reached the ground, they saw a fox running across the yard.

"Look!" Lance said excitedly.

"That's the same one from the other night."

The two watched as the fox paused in the front yard. It looked left and right before running back to the side yard. As it rounded the corner of the house, the fox tumbled.

"I have you now, O' Destructor of Greenery! You shall not foil me again." A spark of green light flew across the yard and landed near the fox.

The two boys jumped back. Near the porch, a man burst from the door wearing white underwear, a ragged T-shirt, and a bathrobe. He strode into the yard holding a sling shot and looked like he hadn't shaved in months, perhaps years. A scraggly beard adorned his chin, and chest hair poked through the various tears in the shirt. His house slippers had Rudolph the Red-Nosed Reindeer where the toes should have been.

"He's the one you're supposed to see?" Lance whispered.

The two boys now crouched behind the fallen tree trunk. The man walked to the fox who lay motionless in the yard. He picked it up by the feet triumphantly. "Never again shall you thwart my gardening plans! I swear, why do I keep you? You are the source of my annoyance." The man held the fox by the tail as he started walking back to the door. He had yet to notice the boys.

"Weird," Lance said to Kyle under his breath.

"Not as weird as that!" Kyle said as the fox sprang to life, curling upward toward its own tail and biting the man on the arm.

He squealed like a young girl as he flapped his hand up and down. The fox fell to the ground with a *thump*. "Curse thee and your buck-toothed venom! I will have vengeance!" The man grabbed a nearby rake and began waving it in the air. The fox ran toward the front gate.

Kyle could not believe what he was watching. He had seen a kraken and a dragon fight and his sister and others be paralyzed, but this scene was just too bizarre. Kyle rubbed his eyes to make sure they were working.

Another green light flashed from the rake and flew over the fox's head. The light hit the padlock on the front gate, sending sparks flying everywhere. The padlock dropped to the ground, and the gate slowly swung open with a loud creak. As it did, the chain-link and privacy fences shortened in height. They were now just three feet or so high, barely above Kyle's waist, and he now had a clear view of the street. The fox looked beyond the gate toward the empty street. It turned to the man, hinting at its next move.

"Be gone with you then," shouted the man. One of the reindeer shoes lit up as he stomped toward the animal. The fox took a few steps onto the street and paused. It issued a squawk that sounded nothing like the noise a fox makes. In the blink of an eye, it spun and began running directly toward Kyle and Lance.

The two boys panicked and scrambled up the fallen tree. Lance slipped, and Kyle reached back to grab Lance's hand. It was too late. They'd been spotted. The fox stopped a few feet in front of Lance. As Lance moved his head, the fox mirrored the motion. The animal raised its ears and began thumping its foot on the ground. Kyle could feel the whole yard shaking.

The man stopped waving the rake. "What? What is it you say?" The man raised his hand to his forehead. He squinted to see the fox and the two boys. "What do we have here?" He walked over to Lance and Kyle. Lance stood up, but did not dare try to climb the tree. The fox stayed in the same spot, beating his foot on the ground. Kyle slid down the trunk to stand beside his friend.

"Who goes there? You!" the man had wild, green eyes and bushy eyebrows. He pointed the rake at Lance. "You! Are you the one who snatched my moment of triumph from this vile creature?"

"N-n-no," Lance stuttered.

Kyle took a step forward, fearing another green bolt would shoot from the rake. "We are sorry. We were just, um..." Kyle didn't know how to finish the sentence, so he just let it drift away.

The fox stopped thumping its foot. It hopped about, acting like a bunny rabbit, then sniffed Kyle's sneakers. It gave two more thumps of its foot before the looking up and mooing.

"Did that fox just moo?" Kyle asked.

He couldn't help himself. He knew he needed to be polite, that he needed to speak with Mr. Olsen and find out who he was and whether the man could help, but Kyle was beginning to doubt that very, very much. He had more important questions to ask than about a mooing fox, but the words had left his lips before he could hold them back.

Strangely, the man seemed unperturbed by the question. "Yes, yes. Don't remind him. He is still all upset about it. A better sound anyway if you ask me. I mean, what sound does a fox utter, anyway?"

Lance started laughing. He hummed under his breath the song, "What does the Fox say!"

Kyle also hummed the song in his head. He couldn't help but give a little chuckle. The man, however, seemed oblivious to the well-known song or that he had just made a joke. The fox walked in a small circle and huffed at the two smiling boys. He let out another "moo," then lifted his nose in contempt and walked away.

Kyle started to talk, but the *My Little Pony* voice came out. "Are you—" He forced a cough and cleared his throat. "Are you Mr. Olsen?"

"Who asks?" The man looked left and right, expecting to see someone else in his yard. "Is this question your own, or has someone manipulated you to come herewith?"

Kyle considered what to say. His story about seeing himself dying in the backyard somehow seemed less strange with a mooing fox and a crazed man swinging a rusty rake. Kyle didn't know how to begin. "Um, I live down the street."

The man stood tall and looked down the street. Then he hunched over again with a finger over his mouth. "Is this about Mrs. Curtis? The lady with the blueish hair? A strange one is she. Very strange. Places her tree clippings in my woods. Thinks I don't know. And she is always reading those colored book pages in her yard."

"Those are Archie comics," Lance said. "I go by there sometimes and she lets me borrow them."

"Stay away from such devilry, my boy!"

Whatever bravo Lance mustered to talk about Archie comics evaporated. He took a step back, bumping into the fallen tree trunk.

Kyle found his resolve. He had come into the yard and met the man. If he was ever going to ask, it had to be now.

"It isn't about Mrs. Curtis. I-I was visited. I was visited by myself. I mean, he looked just like me. Maybe he was me, but me from somewhere else. At least that is what he said. He was dying, and told me to find Merlin." Kyle looked into the man's eyes. There was a bit of madness there, but also a spark. This man was not preparing to laugh at Kyle or send him out of the yard as a trespasser. No, he was listening intently. Kyle pressed on. "He said that I needed to see you. Then, just now on our way here, our school bus was attacked by this kraken thingy. A dragon helped us, but my sister… she is paralyzed. And we—"

"Not here!" the man interrupted, putting a finger to his lips. He looked around as if someone might be spying. Kyle looked too, but there was no one else around. The man waved the rake in the air and the metal prongs lit up with fire. A pale green glow emitted above the flames.

"Come with me." Without waiting, the man ran toward his front door. On the porch, he waved the rake-turned-torch, motioning for the boys to follow.

"We should totally get out of here," Lance said. "There is no way this could get any creepier."

The man gave a whispered yell, the kind that could be heard from afar even though it was in a hushed tone. "Please, come. Hurry." He gave a reassuring smile. "Please, you must. And I have Boysenberry cake and tartar sauce! Come, we must come inside where it is safe." With that, he extinguished the rake by a wave of his hand over the flame.

"Never mind," Lance pronounced. "It just got weirder."

The fox jumped on top of the tree trunk and let out another loud, "Moo."

Kyle took a step toward the door. "You can leave if you want to. I need to know. I saw myself die. My sister might be dead, and that dragon. It won't be able to protect us again if

that thing comes back. And that man knows
something about what's going on.

CHAPTER 18

Two slices of Boysenberry cake were set in front of Kyle and Lance along with a bottle of Fish O' the Sea tartar sauce. Kyle and Lance exchanged uneasy glances as Merle placed a dollop of tartar sauce on his own slice of cake. Kyle decided the best way to avoid eating was to tell the man about his encounter with his dying doppelgänger.

"And this boy, this version of you, said, 'Lynchpin universe?' Are you sure?"

"Positive," Kyle said for the third time. "What does that even mean?"

Merle picked up a sharpie. He searched for a piece of paper but couldn't find one that didn't already have something written on it. In desperation, he went to a birdcage hanging precariously over the kitchen sink and pulled out a white dove. He carried the bird over to the table as it pecked at him to go free. Rather violently, Merle pressed the dove on the table, belly side down. The bird struggled to get free,

164

but the man paid no attention as he began drawing on its back with the sharpie.

"You see, people here have known for a long time there are parallel universes. Who was that wizard? Einstein, I believe? Yes, he was the one who let the proverbial cat out of the bag on that one. It happens in every world eventually. Someone somewhere has a noble idea and suddenly everyone else wants to have an idea, too. They build a bureaucracy to protect their ideas with patents and copyrights, and each thinks his idea is better. Then their ideas start to cause trouble... a virus here, a monster there, a natural catastrophe or a shortage of cabbage and you know what they do?"

Kyle had no idea what they did. A quick glance at Lance suggested Lance didn't either.

"They just make more inventions. They make vaccines, cages, tracking devices, greenhouses, dams, or space stations. Just more of the very same thing that got them into the mess."

Kyle processed this for a moment. In a way, Merle wasn't entirely wrong. Kyle had heard his dad argue that politicians and other elites just made things worse.

"What about video games?" Lance asked. "Those don't hurt anyone."

Kyle waited for him to launch into a tirade like his mom always did about the dangers of video games. What he got instead surprised him.

"Ah! There it is, boy. What is your name?"

"Lance."

Merle tilted his head sideways as if Lance was out of focus before continuing. "Aha! Of course it is. Must be, in fact. You have hit on one thing. Those games keep the truth alive. They teach not only the facts of the universe but how to survive in such. Good stuff they are. Have many myself."

He pointed to his living room where an old, dilapidated camping chair sat in an otherwise empty space facing a large television held up by what seemed to be two petrified racoons. "But those games so often fail in their hubris," he continued. "And the hubris of the matter is what is really important."

"Hubris?" Lance asked.

"Yes. Hubris. The idea that somehow our world is better or at least equal to all the others. The idea that we are the best version of ourselves."

The dove wiggled free and took to the air, but Merle quickly grabbed it by the feet. He set it down on the table again with a thud. The bird's neck extended as the old man flattened out his drawing on the bird's back.

"You see, worlds are grouped together." He drew a flurry of dots on the dove's back. "So while this cluster of worlds all have small deviations, they are all interconnected. And there are a lot of them. Do you know what that means?"

Kyle couldn't help making the snide comment, "It means you have a very unhappy bird?"

"It means that if one world, say this one, goes away it doesn't really impact anything." Merle flipped the sharpie and rubbed the non-writing end on the bird's back. The bird chirped its displeasure. Kyle was about to tell him that the sharpie didn't have an eraser when he realized the dot actually disappeared.

Merle continued, "You can actually lose several of these worlds and everything still holds together." He flipped the bird over and drew dots on its belly as it pecked at his hand. "And there might be a cluster of worlds here as well." He drew groups of dots on the sides and back of the bird, which was starting to resemble a polka-dotted stuffed animal Kyle's sister owned.

The bird pecked Merle's wrist and drew blood. Drops slowly trickled down his wrist and onto the bird's wings. To Kyle and Lance's shock, the blood did not stay in one place. Instead, it shifted into thin red lines that connected the cluster of dots all around the bird. Merle flipped the bird over again, showing the red line running through the initial set of sharpie dots on the other side as well. He drew a large, bold dot near the bird's neck far away from the others.

"Then there are lynchpin worlds. They hold all the other worlds in balance. Like the center hub of a wheel with lots of spokes going outward. Or like a central pole in a tent that holds everything else up. If something goes wrong in one of the clusters, the other worlds balance it out, but the lynchpin worlds hold everything together. And they aren't part of a cluster, you see. They are unique."

"Kind of like this guy," Lance whispered to Kyle.

If the man heard Lance, he made no acknowledgment. Merle continued about the large central dot on the dove. "If a lynchpin world, if one of them disappears..." He again turned the sharpie over and erased the single, bold dot. "…then the connection to all the other worlds falls apart." As the dot magically erased, Kyle and Lance watched all the red lines fade and disappear, then the other dots began to fade as well. The old man held up the bird and shook it like an Etch A Sketch. The drawings vanished. "Understand?"

"If the big dot worlds go away, then it's like cutting a rope that ties the other worlds together?" Lance said hesitantly.

Merle pulled the dove's wings apart, holding a wing tip in each hand. The bird continued to kick its feet and peck at the air. He let go of one of the wings, and the bird swung down, surprised that one wing was no longer being held. As it recovered, it began pecking the hand that continued to hold its other wing. "If the lynchpin world fails, the entire bird, I mean universe, begins to swing out of control. If all lynchpin worlds collapse, then the whole thing collapses into total entropy."

The bird took the opportunity to escape. This time Merle did not try to grab it. The dove flew in circles over their heads until finally a plop of bird poop landed squarely on Merle's half-eaten cake, then returned to the open cage.

"Entropy?" Kyle asked. For a man who wore tattered Rudolph slippers, he sure used a lot of big words.

"Entropy! The movement from order to utter disaster and chaos. And that is where we are headed if we do not do something. You see, your world is in a cluster. Unimportant." He slammed the table, and the plates rose a few inches before clattering back down. "But this visitor, this Kyle from another world, must've been from a lynchpin world." Merle went over to a desk and wrapped his bleeding wrist with a strip of cloth, then he started searching for something. "Funny, though. Funny he should land here, of all worlds."

"What do you mean by that?" Kyle asked.

Merle ignored his question and instead looked down at his half-eaten cake covered with bird poop. He looked over at Kyle's untouched Boysenberry cake. "Are you...?" he asked.

Kyle slid the slice of cake over and the man plopped a dollop of tartar sauce on it.

"So why us? Why here?"

"Yes, funny indeed he would choose here. Things must be dire indeed."

Kyle waited for more, but the man simply began eating his cake. Soon, Lance slid his over as well. When the man was done, he stood and announced, "Outside. We must go outside."

"In your yard?"

"Into another world. We must leave now or all you know in this one will be lost, if it is not already," came Merle's reply.

Kyle felt a lump in his throat and realized it was hard to breathe. In some weird way, he knew what Merle said was true. He knew that he had to go with this eccentric man, and that if he didn't, his family—and his friends—would die. Kyle remembered the words of his doppelgänger:

"If I am not in the lynchpin world, if *you* are not in the lynchpin world, then it falls apart. All worlds fall. Find Merlin. Tell him to take you to the runes. From there, you must travel… to… the…"

Kyle swallowed hard and cleared his throat, then said to Merlin, "Take me to the runes."

EPILOGUE

Gwen turned up the radio while driving on the rural highway. It was currently her favorite pop song, and she wanted one more round of the chorus before she turned the volume down to "mom won't yell at me" levels. She had only been driving a month, and still got the "you better be safe" lectures, but no lecture was going to drown out her mood as Isolde and the Drowning Goldfish sang.

These pathways marked by honest grace,
Take us on a memory trace,
Put on your tinfoil armor, show me the way,
Oh, Oh, we love and fight and love all day.

Gwen didn't notice her speed creeping up as she belted out the chorus. She still had a problem with her right foot pushing a little heavier on the gas pedal when she was distracted. It was for this reason she passed her neighborhood entrance. She watched it pass by, realizing she couldn't stop in time, and was smart enough not to try and turn at full speed.

172

"No worries, I can just turn around at the Dollar Hollar." She continued singing and put her foot back on the gas. Just around the corner was the store and its parking lot.

Gwen never made it to the store. She came around the corner to a sea of blue lights. Cops. Lots of cops. Fire trucks, ambulances. She slammed on the brakes and her SUV went into a spin. There was a screech of the tires as the whole world swirled before the vehicle came to a stop. In front of her was a cop. He was glaring at her just a few inches from her hood. He banged on it with his nightstick and pointed behind her.

"Go back."

Gwen felt her chest tighten as he pointed the stick at her. She was sure she was going to get a ticket or even worse, get arrested. She reached over to turn off the radio. The cop beat on the hood again. He hit it hard enough to leave a small dent. She started to protest but thought better of it.

"Go back," he said again.

She raised her hands, not knowing what else to do.

He walked the few steps to her window, which was already rolled down. Isolde and the

Drowning Goldfish were best played for the world to hear.

"Go back. You can't come through here. Find a different way home."

"My home is just back there. I just missed my turn."

"Not surprised at that," the cop replied. "Slow it down."

She gripped the wheel and put the car in reverse. Still jittery, she pulled into her neighborhood with the radio off. Isolde and the Drowning Goldfish would have to wait until her heart stopped pounding.

Gwen drove along the neighborhood's main thoroughfare. She still had not got used to braking before a turn and the SUV rocked a bit, even now as she was driving much slower. It was something she knew she needed to work on. Gwen slowed the car down a bit, only to take her phone out and start texting.

She had to tell her girlfriends about her near accident with the cops. Not her parents, of course, but her girlfriends needed to know. As she drove past her street sign, Avalon Way, she slammed on her brakes. In her periphery—her dad was always talking about how important peripheral vision was for a young driver—she saw flashing lights in old man Olsen's yard.

Gwen knew he was an oddball, and she had her phone up already to film him.

"Tina, May, Sarah. You aren't going to believe this. Like, I have to tell you. I almost ran over a cop. Like, I am so serious. But first, look. My neighbor."

She switched the camera away from her to film Olsen's yard. There were the usual weird stacks of rocks, but today there was a lot more. His yard was littered with large cardboard boxes, and atop each one was a battery powered strobe light. The boxes were painted gray and there were black streaks in random designs. They almost looked like letters, but nothing she had ever seen before.

Gwen filmed a few seconds and hit send. She was pretty sure he was in his tighty-whities and an old bathrobe. This was too good. She texted:

Want 2 C weird? Look @ this lol.

Gwen put the car in park. She would just step out, take a quick video of whatever madness this was, and jump back inside. She started filming again as she walked closer. Olsen was wearing the Rudolph slippers her family got him for Christmas because, as her mom said, "If we don't give him something, I don't think he'll have anything to open on Christmas morning."

Gwen considered how long ago Christmas was. It was weird he'd still be wearing them, but not as weird as him dancing around waving a torch. He had a real torch, with fire and everything.

She knew this would go viral and make her an instant celebrity, so she couldn't just send it to her friends. No, she would post it on the internet. Old man Olsen wasn't alone. There were two boys with him, and they were tied to the cardboard boxes in the center of the yard. It looked like the cardboard was wrapped around a rather tall tree stump. She paused the video and sent another text.

OMG. I think he kidnapped some1.

Gwen hit send and started filming again. She had visions of instant fame for being the one who caught this on film. A few feet closer, she could see the yard clearly. One of the boys had a fox sitting at his feet as if it was perfectly normal to watch an old man dance around in his underwear while tying boys up in his front yard.

She scanned the yard slowly and tapped the record button to end the video, then posted it to her feed and started filming again. The video

176

started just in time to see old man Olsen high step with his knees and shout, "Oh my goodies!" when part of the torch's flame flickered onto his bathrobe. She sent the new video to her friends, and a few seconds later a text came through from Sarah.

Be careful G!

Gwen decided to go back to her car and call the police, or even drive back to where she had almost run over that officer. After all, there was a bunch of them just a few blocks away. She started to turn back to her SUV and the old man spoke loudly, saying something she knew wasn't English.

This guy is absolutely crazy, she thought. She started to get a feeling that she needed to move quicker, that the two boys might be in real trouble. His voice grew deeper. It didn't just sound weird, it sounded scary. She thought about her post. She didn't want to have to tell someone she saw these boys get killed and all she did was post a video of it. She decided to act immediately and dialed 911.

"911, what's your emergency?"

"Yes, um, I am on Avalon Way. Like, almost to my house. There is a man here. He has two boys tied up in his yard."

"Ma'am, did you say he has two boys tied up in his yard?"

"Yes, to trees, I think. Like trees covered in cardboard boxes."

"Ma'am? We have a lot of activity out that way. You aren't kidding me, right?"

"No, ma'am."

"OK. I'll see if I can get someone there. Ma'am are you in a safe—"

The phone went dead in her ear. She pulled it away and looked at it. Gwen pressed the home button several times and breathed a sigh of relief when the little icon indicating it restarted showed up in the middle of the screen. Gwen dialed 911 again. She looked at the screen and saw the *Call Failed* notice.

The kids yelled, and she recognized their voices. It was Kyle and Lance. A part of her told her to run to her SUV and get to safety. The other part urged her to run toward Olsen's yard, and sprinted forward, yelling, "Hey! You! I called the cops. You can't tie up—"

The fox ran up to her, looping around her legs so it could run alongside her. It opened its mouth and mooed at her. Gwen screamed, stepping sideways. She stumbled and staggered forward, trying to regain her balance, but she crashed into Olsen's front gate. It swung open as she hit it, and she tumbled into the yard. She looked up and saw Kyle. He was bound to a tree and a battery powered strobe light flashed over his head.

Lightning flashed, and Gwen felt heat all around her as bolts of lightning crashed down across the yard. One of the trees fell, blocking the entrance gate. She could barely see her SUV through the branches. Another tree fell, then another.

Glancing around, Gwen saw the trees had fallen in a perfect formation, forming a wall around her, Olsen, and the two boys. The fox ran out from one of the fallen trees with a biscuit in its mouth. There was another flash of light, and that was the last thing Gwen saw on her own world.

The adventure continues with
Lynchpin Universe: The Sword in the Kraken

The Author

Jerry is the author of Middle Grade and Young Adult works including Freckles: The Dark Wizard and the award-winning Jam Sessions.

When not writing, Jerry teaches both Middle School ELA and as an adjunct psychology professor.

He lives in Sale Creek, TN with his amazing wife and French Bulldog. He has six kids, but most of them are now "adulting." Jerry hopes to "adult" someday, too.